The Vine Church

Eturuvie Erebor

A DOZ Chronicles Drama

ISBN: 978-1-8383844-8-7

THE VINE CHURCH

Copyright ©2025 Eturuvie Erebor

Published in London, England by Eturuvie Erebor trading as DOZ Chronicles, a unit of DOZ Network.

All rights reserved, including the right of reproduction in whole or in part in any form. No person, organisation or party may copy, reproduce, communicate, circulate, or translate the content or images in this publication without the express written consent of the publisher and or author.

This is a work of fiction. The characters, names, locations, places, and events are purely fictional. They bear no connection to any actual persons, living or dead, or any real places, business establishments, locations, happenings, or incidents. Any resemblance is wholly coincidental.

Behind the polished oak doors of The Vine Church, three prayers rise to heaven.

Victoria Griffith prays for her husband's attention.

Mabel Babs-Jonah prays for another woman's life.

And Elizabeth David-West prays that her sins won't destroy them all.

At the altar stands Pastor John Griffith—a shepherd whose own flock might just lead him astray. His sermons speak of divine love, but his wife, Victoria, knows that even God's servants can forget how to love what's right in front of them. When Mabel, raw from abandonment and hungry for belonging, fixes her eyes on the good pastor, she sees not just a man of God, but a chance at the life she covets.

But it's Elizabeth, the pastor's own sister, who might strike the match that sets their carefully constructed world up in flames. She's trapped in a crumbling marriage and tangled in an affair with Barry—the same man whose departure shattered Mabel's family.

As these three families with all-too-human hearts merge, the church itself becomes the battlefield. Will they come out of it with their faith intact, or will it destroy the foundation of everything they hold sacred? In the end, grace may be their only salvation—but only if they can find it in time.

Dear Reader,

I have been waiting ten years to bring this book to you. The story's presentation isn't as I expected, but the story's being told, and that's what's important. In 2015, a producer friend requested a Christian fiction story for a movie, prompting the creation of this story. The friend in question had just produced her first movie and desired to make a second one.

This story marked my first attempt at scriptwriting. Unfortunately, my friend never got to read the script. Certain personal events meant that once the story was finished, she couldn't read it, let alone work with it.

The story remained abandoned and forgotten until about April 2024, when I stumbled upon it. Once I read it, I realised it wasn't too bad and could be written as a novel. I thought I would give it the kiss of life with a little tweaking. It required more than a little tweaking. Major changes to the story were made, and the writing and editing process took longer than I expected, but I have no regrets. It's currently a fantastic story, and I'm grateful God chose me to write it.

The Vine Church is finally here, not as a movie but as a novel. I hope you enjoy reading it. I have certainly enjoyed the long hours of writing and rewriting the story.

Please send me your comments and feedback. You can write to me through my website, www.eturuvieerebor.com, or email eturuvie@eturuvieerebor.com.

I look forward to hearing from you.

Evie.

For Jesus

PROLOGUE

Manchester, United Kingdom…14 Months Ago

Barry Babs-Jonah pulled out his phone, which vibrated softly in his winter fleece leather jacket pocket. Even before he answered the call, he sensed it was the cab he had booked to take him to the airport for his trip to Lagos. No one else would be calling him this early in the morning.

"Good morning." He spoke softly so as not to wake his family, still in bed. "Drive up to the front of the house and wait for me. I'll be out in a few minutes."

Barry moved swiftly but quietly through the quiet and dark house with only a lamp on the console in the hallway to guide him. From the guest bedroom downstairs, which doubled as his home office, and where he spent most of the night packing, he carried his suitcases into the hallway.

Finished, he sat at his desk and wrote a letter to his wife asleep in their upstairs bedroom. His wife and daughters remained ignorant of his plans and would wake in a few hours to find him absent, not only from the home but also from their lives.

He paused his writing and pinched the bridge of his nose. His marriage wasn't as he'd envisioned, yet that was reality, and he refused to manage it any longer. Barry was a prosperous Yoruba businessman in his late forties. He left Lagos for the United Kingdom twenty years ago, seeking greener pastures; his search, as well as hard work, paid off.

His business exported African food products worldwide. Two years ago, he diversified into property and owned an impressive portfolio of commercial and residential properties in the UK, Lagos, and Dubai. Shortly after relocating to the UK, he married and brought a woman from his tribe to live with him in Lagos.

He held high hopes and dreams for them as a couple. His plan was to fund her schooling to a doctoral degree. He envisioned them as a power couple. But Mabel had other plans. She desired many children; two quick births later, she deemed a college degree enough, forgoing further education.

When the third child arrived, she believed that being a housewife and mother constituted her life's ambition. Disappointment washed over him. He had an MBA. Relating with her didn't work. But she didn't understand and assumed he nagged unnecessarily. Moreover, she put on so much weight, and with every passing year, he found her less and less attractive and stopped sleeping with her.

He quickly realised that with the kind of success he had attained, and as he was a big spender, getting a woman outside to appear attractive for him and give him great sex was as easy as pie. He threw himself into countless affairs with sugar babies, taking them with him when he travelled abroad and enjoying their beautiful presence and beautiful bodies. But he quickly became bored as the girls, while looking better than Mabel, shared a similar IQ that made it difficult to hold any meaningful conversation with them.

Two years ago, when he began his property business, he met a beautiful solicitor in London—a woman with intelligence that matched her beauty. She was everything he'd hoped Mabel would be. It started as just business as she handled the conveyancing for the properties he purchased within the UK. But after several months of business lunches, their attraction for one another became evident, and a relationship developed.

They made the perfect power couple. He brought her sufficient business and helped her become a partner in her firm, and she helped him acquire numerous properties in a short time. The longer he stayed with her, the harder it was to return home to Mabel with her big body and small mind and be content. The fact that she wasn't religious and didn't constantly discuss church and Jesus enhanced her appeal. He heard enough of that at home.

Mabel incessantly discussed it; perhaps because she lacked comprehension concerning politics, finance, and business. Furthermore, his new partner was adventurous in bed and willing to try things Mabel wouldn't even hear about. And unlike Mabel, she constantly sought to spice up their sex life, introducing new things to the bedroom, and he looked forward with anticipation to every business trip he took with her. After their last trip, he decided to leave Mabel. She and the kids would be well provided for to maintain their current lifestyle. He owed them that much. He concluded that covered his entire obligation to them.

Once finished, he put the letter in an envelope, sealed it and left it on the kitchen counter where he thought she'd easily find it. He left the kitchen and crept up the carpeted stairs, looking into the bedroom where his wife slept and then peering into the bedrooms where his daughters soundly slept. With hands buried deep inside the pockets of his trousers, he lingered for a while in deep reflection and then quickly pulled himself out of his daydream and returned downstairs. His suitcases were in the hallway where he'd left them, and he picked them up and walked out, shutting the door quietly behind him.

The house remained quiet long after his departure. Inside the main bedroom, only the quiet breathing of the woman sleeping on the super king-sized bed and nestled under the luxurious eiderdown duvet was perceptible. Suddenly, the digital alarm clock on the bedside table beeped, bringing the quietness to an end. From under the duvet, Mabel Babs-Jonah turned it off.

"Not another Monday morning," she moaned.

Mabel, a woman in her early forties, was a devoted mother to her three daughters. However, she lacked the motivation and energy to care for them or her home and constantly required the help of cleaners and au pairs, although she was a full-time stay-at-home mum.

She turned towards her husband, wishing to cuddle and gather the strength to leave the bed. As she inched closer to him, she noticed the empty coldness of his side of the bed. She sat, surveying her surroundings, searching for him. He worked late into the night in his home office downstairs, which meant he was fast asleep when she got up to prepare the kids for school. She looked towards the bathroom.

"Babe?" she called out, but received no response. She got out of bed and put on her dressing gown. The bathroom door remained shut but unlocked; opening it, she found no trace of him.

"Strange," she muttered under her breath. Whatever got him out of bed this early must be urgent and important.

Perhaps he slept off downstairs, she thought.

Immediately, she dismissed the thought; that behaviour was uncharacteristic of him. Besides, his side of the bed looked slept in, so he most likely went out early.

She focused on getting the children ready for school. As she entered the bedroom of her eldest, Tracy, she groaned, taking in the sight before her. The fourteen-year-old's belongings were scattered everywhere.

"Time to call in the cleaners," she murmured as she picked up some clothes and dumped them on the armchair by the bed.

The cleaners came around only the day before. At this rate, she would probably get them to come in daily. Maybe she'd benefit from hiring a live-in housekeeper. Her last au pair quit before Christmas, and the girls needed someone to mind them when they returned from school and prepare them for school.

Not being a morning person, rising early to prepare the girls for school took its toll on her. Yes, a housekeeper to clean, cook and care for the girls would greatly benefit her. She experienced some difficulty waking Tracy, a deep sleeper, but at last, after she awoke, she left her to go into Stacy's room. Thirteen-year-old Stacy slept a lot lighter than her older sister. The instant Mabel entered the room, the teen lifted her sleep mask and stretched under her duvet.

"Is it morning, Mummy?"

"Yes, it's morning," Mabel said. "You need to get up and get in the bathroom."

Knowing that Stacy would not return to sleep, she moved towards the bedroom of six-year-old Daisy—but only after looking in again on Tracy. Just as she feared, Tracy was back in bed and fast asleep. She sighed. Preparing the kids for school involved a significant amount of effort. She must get that housekeeper immediately, she decided as she pulled a grumbling Tracy out of bed, and led her to the bathroom before entering Daisy's bedroom.

Like a cherub, chubby-cheeked Daisy looked at Mabel over her duvet; Mabel smiled. She and Barry produced beautiful children.

She bent and kissed a round cheek. "Get up. It's time to get ready for school."

With the children out of bed, she proceeded to the kitchen, switching on the light. Her eyes caught sight of an envelope on the kitchen worktable, and she frowned. That wasn't there when she turned in last night. It bore her name and the handwriting she instantly recognised as her husband's. Still frowning, she reached out and took it. Her hands trembled slightly as she opened the envelope and took out the letter. Although unaware of the contents, she sensed it wasn't good news. She sighed deeply as she began to read.

My dearest Mabel, you are probably wondering where I am. I wish to put your heart at rest, hence this letter. I will get straight to the point without wasting your time. It is over between us. I have decided to leave you. Over the last year, I have travelled more and worked longer into the nights, mainly to avoid spending time with you. Your inability to develop yourself has informed my decision to move on. I am gone; by the time you read this, I should be at the airport and on my way to Lagos. Please do not try to contact me, as my phone will be switched off. Barry.

Engrossed in reading, Mabel didn't hear Tracy enter the kitchen. Then she looked up, wide-eyed, as Tracy asked, "Mum, are you all right?"

Mabel didn't answer but stared straight ahead, looking at nothing in particular and seeing nothing at all. Then, her legs buckled under her, and she dropped to the kitchen floor. As darkness enveloped everything, she heard Tracy scream.

"Mum!"

CHAPTER ONE

London, United Kingdom… Today

"Who will tell me what lessons they learnt from last Sunday's sermon?"

Pastor John Griffith, a tall, handsome man with a strong, formidable personality, reclined in his favourite armchair in the family living room, his sock-clad feet propped on the footstool. Opposite him, his family sat on the spacious and plump mustard velvet sofa. He raised a brow as he looked from his wife to their children, anticipating an answer to his question. He led the Saturday evening family Bible study before retiring to his home office to study, pray, and meditate in preparation for the service the following day.

Pastor John, affectionately called that by everyone familiar with him, was the senior pastor and founder of The Vine Church, a megachurch with ten thousand members in the Hampstead area of North London. His parents would be proud. They were white British missionaries who spent most of their lives in South Africa planting churches until they drew their last breath five years ago within days of each other. John and his sister,

Elizabeth, several years his junior, were born and raised in South Africa.

John loved the Lord and his work as a pastor, although shepherding a large church meant he didn't get to spend as much time with his family as he would have liked. His wife, Victoria, raised the kids almost alone as he transitioned from being a part-time doctor and part-time pastor to a full-time pastor, growing the church and caring for the flock.

"I am surprised that no one can tell me what lessons they learnt from last Sunday's sermon," he said. "Okay, let me change the question. Who recalls the subject of last Sunday's sermon?"

Again, he looked from his wife to their three children, wondering why they looked morose, like the meeting was unfamiliar and unscheduled. Saturday evening Bible study occurred regularly. He hadn't participated in a while, but Victoria always held the session with the children and shared briefly with him their discussions, which always revolved around the previous Sunday's sermon.

"Victoria?" he asked with a raised brow. Surely, his own wife remembered his sermon?

Victoria Griffith folded her hands in her lap and pursed her lips. She was a petite, reserved woman in her mid-forties, and although beautiful, with auburn hair and green eyes, she battled low self-esteem. Over the years, her more intelligent, attractive, and arrogant husband subjected her to browbeating and suppressed her into resignation. He was the perfect Christian who demanded the perfect marriage, home, and children. It seemed her singular responsibility to provide these while he gave his time and energy to the church and its members.

This will be tricky, she considered as she tried to remember John's message preached the Sunday before.

She hoped one of the children remembered and said something to help jog her memory because the harder she thought, the more she drew blanks. It had been a busy week, managing the kids, attending a meeting with Paul's teacher, taking John Jr. to his appointments with the doctor and dentist and driving Rebekah to a university open evening. Besides, when she held these sessions with the kids, they looked up the message on the church's website and then discussed it. As the kids remained silent, she offered a suggestion.

"Perhaps someone could check the church's website for it?" She turned to John Jr. and Rebekah, sitting to her right.

"What do you mean, check the church's website?" John sounded displeased. "Is that how you've been running these sessions, Victoria?"

Victoria opened her mouth to speak, but thought better of it. John would not hear her explanations and would accuse her of losing her zeal for the things of God.

"It's only been a few days. Less than a week." His look of disapproval rested on her briefly before it shifted to the kids. "Come on, guys. What was the message, and what did you learn from it?" He looked at John Jr. and Rebekah.

Victoria stifled a sigh. Although she wanted her husband to spend more time with her and their children, this one time, she wished he'd been occupied with one of his many responsibilities and left her to run the session. She couldn't remember his message, and apparently, neither could the children, or they would have said something by now. She didn't remember when any of them recalled John's message without consulting the church's website.

The children probably had a different reason for not remembering their father's sermon. Her reason was that she was distracted and paid little attention when John stood at the pulpit to preach. He was a handsome man in his late forties with a great body, and he looked like a Greek god in his expensive three-piece Saville Row suits and handmade Italian shoes. His voice made women go weak at the knees, and he didn't have to try.

The women at church loved him. She saw it in their eyes. When he climbed the altar to preach, they looked at him like they wanted to devour him. Single and married women alike. Yes. And they looked at her with a combination of envy and contempt. They envied her, assuming she led a life of ease from marrying such a stunning, godly man; they also believed John represented everything they desired in a partner, and she was the lucky one enjoying all they craved.

Publicly, he showed great care. He cared for his church members and constantly supported them during their hardships. He was a wealthy man who made some good investments when he transitioned from being a medical doctor to being a full-time pastor. His investments yielded returns, and he showed extreme generosity to the church members, especially single mothers striving independently to raise their children.

If only they understood that she wasn't as fortunate as they believed. If only they realised that her husband spread himself so thin doing God's work and serving the various families in the church that he had nothing left at the end of each day to give to her and their children. They assumed that because John spent time with them, he did the same with his wife. But he didn't. She was a lonely woman who longed for more time with her husband and wanted romance and affection.

John showed affection only when he wanted sex; his departure after intimacy left her feeling used and cheap. She raised the issue once, and John accused her of being a selfish woman who resented the time her husband invested in helping other less fortunate families. He reminded her that she surpassed the single women he aided because she had a husband and enjoyed considerable financial security.

She clammed up because he didn't get her. He didn't understand a woman's needs, although anyone watching his interactions with the women at church would say the opposite. And when she heard him advise husbands, Victoria wished he took half of that advice and implemented it in their marriage and family.

"I can't believe this!" John glared at his family.

How was this even possible? he wondered.

How was it that none of the members of his immediate family recalled what sermon he'd preached on Sunday? He preached the message only six days ago. Six days, and they'd forgotten? He wagered that a call to any church member would reveal his sermon topic. They'd remember because they paid attention. He was well-loved by his church members. They hung on to every word he said so they'd remember. Yet, his own wife and children couldn't recollect.

"Okay. Do you want to consult your notes to see if perhaps that will jog your memories?"

Victoria looked guilty as she looked from one child to another, and the children looked uncomfortable.

"I'm sorry, Dad, but my notes must have been deleted from my iPad, possibly because I failed to save them. Right after the sermon, they disappeared completely."

Rebekah Griffith broke the awkward silence, her heart racing in her chest. The eighteen-year-old with long blond hair and blue eyes looked stunning, like her aunt Elizabeth, and reminded John of his errant sister each time he looked at her. She chewed nervously on her bottom lip and hoped her father would accept her explanation and not pursue the matter further.

The entire meeting looked as if she stood at the gates of heaven, awaiting an angel to determine her eternity's destination. She wished some church-related emergency would emerge and take her father away as it always did.

"That was careless, Rebekah. More so because you should have remedied the situation immediately by taking someone else's notes or going to the website, as your mother earlier suggested, which seems to be the practice in my absence."

Rebekah shifted in her seat, a flicker of guilt washing over her features. Her unease was evident, and the reason for it was simple. Rebekah took no notes during the service in question. She spent most of the sermon chatting with her boyfriend, Conor. Conor Wilson, a professional footballer, was a few years her senior. As he was neither a member of The Vine Church nor a Christian, Rebekah kept him a secret. During the service, she texted Conor using her iPad. Parishioners watching her assumed she took notes of the sermon or looked up the Bible passages as they were stated, but the entire time, she did anything but that.

"Sorry, Dad," Rebekah muttered. "I'll do better next time."

"As you should," John admonished. "The entire church congregation looks up to me and my family. How can I stand at the pulpit and ask people to take notes of the sermon if my family isn't taking notes?"

Victoria looked away. Like Rebekah, she had no notes, as she usually doodled absentmindedly on her iPad while John preached. She prayed John didn't ask to see her notes. As she struggled to come up with a solid explanation for why she was missing her notes, John suddenly broke into her thoughts, pulling her back to the present.

"And before we proceed, who approved using iPads instead of notebooks and pens?"

"You did, Dad," Rebekah said before Victoria responded.

John sighed and shook his head. "I don't remember, and I don't want to get into that now." He looked at Victoria. "I won't be asking about your notes now, Victoria."

Her sigh of relief was almost detectible as John turned away from her and looked at his older son. John Jr. shrugged carelessly to indicate his lack of notes. John frowned.

What was going on?

"What's your excuse?" he asked.

"I worked with the ushering team during the sermon," was his excuse.

"That's nonsense. I'm certain that if I called up an ushering team member now, they would share the sermon and their notes with me. You are a disgrace."

John Jr., a seventeen-year-old boy much like his father in looks and temperament, was probably the only person in the family who did not cringe or run and hide when John descended on the family and bellowed at them in displeasure. He shrugged once again, unperturbed by the fact that he'd been called a disgrace. Unlike Rebekah, he did not apologise for failing to have any notes.

John sighed and ran a hand through his blond hair, emphasising the attractive grey streak. This wasn't acceptable. He looked at the youngest of his children, Paul. He didn't expect Paul to remember if the older children and his wife didn't.

"Paul, you wouldn't happen to know what Daddy preached last Sunday, would you?"

Paul shook his head. "No, Daddy. I'm sorry."

John smiled at his youngest to reassure him. At seven years of age, Paul was an intelligent boy, shy in public and boisterous at home. He typically finished Sunday school and joined the main service as the sermon began, and preferred to sit quietly at the back and watch cartoons on his device. His father would never have allowed it, insisting that he listen to the sermon even if he couldn't comprehend it, but his mother permitted it so he wouldn't be bored.

"In the future, Victoria, I want you to check that the kids have their notes from service. You will do this on Sundays after dinner before bedtime and report to me, and while you do, I will also check that you have your notes. Do you understand?"

"Yes, John." Victoria grinned. "So, will you refresh our memories about the sermon?"

John studied his wife, and although many things came to mind that he wanted to say to her, he held his tongue. They were in the presence of the children. But he made a mental note to have a conversation with her later. He didn't know what she was thinking, letting things slide in the home. She'd been mad at him years ago when he didn't appoint her the women's leader in the church.

Still, he did it because he doubted her ability to manage the large group of women in the church, and he refused to inflate her ego by giving her a position she believed she deserved but which they both knew she wasn't mature enough to handle. Now, she made him doubt her ability to handle herself without supervision, let alone three children, never mind the over five thousand women in the church.

"Of course." His smile did not reach his eyes. "Last week Sunday, I preached on discerning the will of God."

"Ah, yes, I remember," Rebekah said.

John pressed his lips together. "I'm glad you do, Rebekah," he muttered drily. "So, are you going to be the first to tell us what lessons you took away from the sermon?"

Just as Rebekah opened her mouth, John's phone rang. John sighed as he picked up the phone from the stool beside his chair. It was Chris, his sister, Elizabeth's husband.

"Yes, Chris, this is John. What's going on?"

A few minutes later, he rose from his seat as he ended the call. He smiled apologetically at Victoria. "I'm sorry, but you must take over the Bible study. I need to see Elizabeth and Chris."

CHAPTER TWO

Chris David-West picked up the last suitcase and carried it down the stairs. He was a handsome man of African descent in his mid-forties. Quiet and peace-loving, he was the opposite of his wife, Elizabeth. When they first married, he owned a thriving business. David-West, his company, developed commercial and residential real estate in West Africa, primarily in his hometown of Port-Harcourt.

Four years ago, he fell on hard times when the David-West Tower, the highest residential building his company ever constructed, collapsed, killing almost a hundred people. Because his son James was in Port-Harcourt, and the nanny called to say James was throwing up his food, he was spared the same fate. The building collapsed just after he left the site to go home and check on James.

Money passed hands under the table to keep him out of prison, and more money was paid out to compensate the victims' families. It marked the end for David-West. He suffered a heart attack brought on by shock and spent weeks in the hospital. Afterwards, he battled depression and lost the will and drive to try again, content to stay home and care for their two boys. James and Andrew.

A year and a half ago, he started purchasing dilapidated houses, renovating them personally, and then selling them. Though the profit margin was small in comparison with his past ventures, he found the hands-on work healing. The work also allowed him to spend time with his sons and care for them, working around their needs, while Elizabeth pursued her career as a solicitor and became a partner in her firm.

He loved his wife and wanted to support her in achieving her dream in every way possible. But he doubted he could return to being the man he once was. Elizabeth wanted a man wearing a power suit and going to a big office daily. Once, he'd been that man; now, he was the man who wore coveralls, drove a van and worked with his hands to repair rundown houses. He was happy with the status quo and was amazed that his wife wasn't.

He was a good provider, and his family didn't lack despite his past predicament. True, he couldn't give Elizabeth diamond jewellery and watches, and she couldn't go to Knightsbridge and splurge with his credit card as she'd frequently done in the past. But their needs were met. He managed to save their six-bedroom Hampstead home, and they could still send their children to an independent school, change their cars and travel; this was more than many in the country could afford, and he believed they should be thankful.

Elizabeth judged differently and saw what she termed his lack of ambition as a reason for them to part ways and end their marriage. She asked him to move out. He was doing just that. But not before her brother arrived. Pastor John Griffith was their pastor and Elizabeth's older brother, and Chris hoped he would intervene. As he turned to go back upstairs, the doorbell rang. He moved towards the front door, and simultaneously, Elizabeth stepped out of the study.

At forty-one years of age, Elizabeth David-West was a remarkable and highly ambitious woman. As a successful conveyancing solicitor with long blonde hair, blue eyes, and the tall, lean body of a model, she was a perfect combination of beauty and brains. She was the mother of two boys, but no one would guess just by looking at her. Although it was a Saturday evening and she spent the day at home working, she was stylishly dressed in coffee-coloured skinny leather pants, a cream chunky mohair jumper, and Micheal Kors suede platform boots.

Elizabeth was aware of her beauty and did not hesitate to flaunt it, flirting her way through the corridors of power and wealth. Her beauty removed her from the impoverished life her missionary parents plunged her into at birth. She grew up poor and came to resent her parents and their God. She abhorred lack and any appearance of it and, as such, she was highly impatient with her husband, constantly nagging him to quit playing small.

"Don't worry, I'll get it." She dismissed him with a wave as she moved towards the front door to open it.

"It's John," he said.

Elizabeth paused at the door and turned to glare at him. "Did you ask him over?"

Chris suspected she was about to go into one of her tirades, telling him off like he was James or Andrew.

"Elizabeth, just open the door, please."

She gave him a disapproving glance before turning to open the door. Chris sighed again, wondering how he had failed to see this side of Elizabeth seventeen years ago when he asked her to marry him. He wondered how she would cope with James and Andrew when he was gone. Andrew was not so much a handful. At six, he stayed out of trouble, content to watch television. James was a different kettle of fish altogether. At sixteen, he was an extrovert who liked to party and hang out with friends. He required continuous supervision; his adventurous nature made him prone to mishaps.

Elizabeth opened the door, and as Chris predicted, it was John. She knew why Chris invited him over. It was Chris's way of getting John to talk her into carrying on with the marriage. Still, her mind was made up, and as much as she loved and respected John, there was no way she would let him dictate to her how to live her life; it was her life, after all.

Chris was a good man, but she didn't love him anymore; everyone should respect that. Her affections lay elsewhere, with a man of means. The man in question, Barry Babs-Jonah, was a moneyed client of hers. She met him about three years ago when he visited her office, requiring conveyancing services for some houses he sought to purchase. He was everything she desired in a man: focused, enterprising, and extremely ambitious.

Elizabeth spent much time with him under the guise of work. So far, she'd accompanied him on business trips to America, Asia, and the Middle East. Chris assumed the trips were work-related. Barry left his wife last year and moved from Manchester to London, and for her, it signalled his readiness to take their relationship further. She stopped sleeping with Chris last year and asked him to move into another bedroom. But it was time to be properly separated from him.

She dragged herself back to the present as she stepped back into the hall, allowing her brother to enter and forcing a smile to form around her lips.

"Hello, brother dearest." She was a little tense as she embraced him and kissed his cheek.

"Hello, Elizabeth. How are you?" John withdrew from the embrace to regard her, scanning her well-groomed hair, made-up face, and designer casual wear. For someone who was planning to end her marriage, she looked well, he admitted to himself.

"I'm as well as can be expected, thank you," she said, manoeuvring around him to close the front door.

Chris was standing in the middle of the foyer, at the foot of the stairs, his hands buried deep inside the pockets of his non-iron chinos. John glanced at the three suitcases by the staircase and wondered why Chris called him to intervene, seeing as he was already packed to leave. Perhaps it was because he knew his wife well enough to know that not even her older brother could convince her to continue the marriage. Inviting John over was a step toward fulfilling all righteousness.

"Hey, Chris. How are you?"

John walked over to him, extending his hand as he did.

"I'm good, John. Thanks for coming over and at such short notice."

"Anytime, Chris."

He made eye contact for a few seconds, and Chris looked away, but not before John saw the pain buried deep inside those expressive eyes.

John liked Chris and figured he was a great guy, although he always doubted his suitability for a woman like Elizabeth. John loved his sister dearly, but wondered how Chris put up with her. She was domineering and manipulative. If she wasn't in control, she wanted out; however, if allowed to have control, she grew tired of the man, lost all respect for him and wanted out.

John watched their relationship from the sidelines for many years. Initially, all seemed fine; not due to Elizabeth's regard for Chris—she never respected him—but because Chris possessed considerable wealth and could provide Elizabeth with the luxuries she deeply desired. However, when Chris suffered a major setback, everything changed, and the real Elizabeth emerged.

"Shall we talk in the living room?" Chris asked, pointing toward the room to his right, which had a big double door wide open.

Elizabeth preceded both men into the large and comfortable room with its beautiful floral arrangements and brightly coloured sofas, throw pillows, and a lovely display of family photos on the mantelpiece. She sat down, crossing her long, shapely legs as she did. Chris sat in an armchair, leaving John to sit next to Elizabeth on the sofa.

John looked towards the foyer and Chris's suitcases and was about to ask why Chris called him, seeing as he intended to leave. But as he opened his mouth to speak, Elizabeth interrupted him.

"John, you're probably wondering why you were asked over and frankly, so am I." She sounded like she was trying hard to suppress her frustration with the situation. "I would not have dragged you into this. This is between Chris and me. We're both adults and have made a decision; everyone should respect that decision. You're my older brother, and I respect you a great deal, but my decision to separate from Chris is final; I've given great thought to it and decided it is best for me and the kids and, of course, Chris, that we both go our separate ways. Chris hasn't tried to get back on his feet since losing his business. He's doing menial work in rundown houses as a plumber, carpenter and painter. Instead of rebuilding his business empire, he drives a ridiculous van like a typical blue-collar worker. I'm becoming frustrated living with a man who doesn't aspire for more out of life.

"Chris supported me in becoming who I am today; he looked after the kids to allow me to focus on my career. I'm grateful, but cannot stay with him on those grounds. You probably think that as a missionary's daughter and a pastor's sister, I shouldn't divorce, but I have my own life to live. I'm not a missionary or a pastor; I'm Elizabeth, a solicitor. You probably also think I'm not being fair to Chris, especially since he had a hard time with his health following the setback in his business, but I think he's had ample time to get over it and move on, but he refuses to. I want a husband I can be proud of, and I'm not proud of

Chris. I no longer respect him, and I no longer love him. It's over for me."

When she finished speaking, the living room became hushed, so quiet that the sound of a pin dropping onto the soft yellow patterned carpet would have been heard. Chris avoided looking at John before, but now, it was John who avoided looking at Chris. He pitied the man and, not for the first time, realised that Chris would be better off starting a new life without Elizabeth in it. Yes, she was his sister, and he loved her, but she was a wife he would not wish on any man. John wondered why Chris hadn't left her before now and waited to be kicked out of her life.

"So, now that you've decided to end your marriage, what will happen to your sons? Have you considered them, Elizabeth, or is it all about what you want?"

"This is my life, John, in case you forgot. The kids have their lives."

She was determined that no one, not even her children, would stop her from ending her marriage to Chris. If he wanted to be poor, she wanted no part of it. She married Chris because he was thriving. After watching her parents struggle financially, she decided to marry well. Once she left South Africa for Britain to attend university, she realised she was beautiful, and men would do anything to be with her.

She swiftly adopted the lifestyle of a sugar baby, dating older affluent men who gave her luxuries beyond her parents' means. Chris took her away from that life, but if he imagined he was capable of trapping her and making her live without the finer things because he was unwilling to rebuild his business, he was in for a shock. The kids were in for a shock. Everyone was in for a shock.

"They have their lives," John repeated her words and reflected on them momentarily, nodding in agreement. "The boys will lead their own lives someday, but for now, their lives are tied to yours. Have you considered how this will affect them?"

"Of course, I have, which is why I've decided they'll live with me. Chris, of course, can see them whenever he wants to, and they can stay with him when I'm away on business."

"And this is okay?" John asked.

Elizabeth frowned, not quite sure what he meant. "Yes, it's okay. Chris and I agreed that this was how it would be, and we informed the boys. Naturally, they weren't pleased with the arrangement, but like I said, it's my life, my marriage, and if I say I've had enough, everyone should respect that."

He slowly got to his feet, sighing, and shaking his head. His eyes flickered between Elizabeth and Chris before he silently headed for the front door.

Elizabeth was the first to react. "Wh-Where are you going?" she asked. "Aren't you going to say anything?"

John stopped and turned back to look at them. They both stood and appeared shocked by his actions. He smiled, shaking his head.

"Nah, I'm not going to say anything," he said, locking eyes with Elizabeth. "You've said it all. You've figured everything out." He turned and opened the front door, walking out and shutting it behind him before they stopped him.

Elizabeth was the first of the two to recover. She turned on Chris angrily. "Well, what was the point in inviting John over? What good did it do? Did it solve anything?"

Chris shrugged. "Perhaps the point was not to solve anything. I doubt you can be convinced when your mind is made up."

Elizabeth raised a brow as she folded her arms across her chest. "When you know this to be true, why did you ask John over?"

"Just drop it, Elizabeth. Maybe a tiny part of me that still loves you and wants this marriage to work hoped you'd listen to John. But your mind is made up; it couldn't have been more apparent as you spoke to John."

He walked towards his suitcases, and just then, the front door opened, and James and Andrew came rushing in, to Chris's utter surprise and Elizabeth's annoyance. Earlier that day, Elizabeth asked a friend of hers, Anita, to take the boys to her home for the day so they wouldn't be home when their dad left. The plan was unsuccessful; the boys' timely arrival coincided with Chris's exit.

"Dad!" they chorused in unison and ran into Chris's arms.

Anita, a stunning mixed-race woman in her early forties, gazed into the house through the open door. She was Elizabeth's best friend and also a solicitor. Unlike Elizabeth, Anita specialised in criminal law. Both women worked together and were partners in the large solicitor's firm, where they had worked since qualifying fifteen years ago. A single mum of Sophie, aged fourteen, and Matthew, aged nine, she sometimes included James and Andrew in family outings.

Anita grinned apologetically, first at Chris and then at Elizabeth. "I'm sorry, but they insisted they wanted to return home. Andrew was already starting to throw a tantrum."

Elizabeth looked at Andrew and wagged a finger before turning to Anita. "It's always the little one," she said, rolling her blue eyes. "Don't worry about it, Anita. Thank you for watching them."

"I need to go," Anita said. "Sophie and Matthew are in the car."

"Thank you, Anita." Chris extricated himself from the boys, walked closer to Anita, and shook her hand. "Drive carefully."

"I will do. Good night." Anita turned to Elizabeth. "Walk me to my car?"

"Of course," Elizabeth responded and walked out after Anita, leaving Chris alone with the boys.

"Daddy, don't go. Andrew will be a good boy," Andrew pleaded, grabbing Chris's legs, and looking up at him pleadingly.

Chris gently removed his hands so that he might squat to his level. "Hey, little man, we've talked about this. Dad is still going to be around, only…"

"Not in this house." James finished the sentence drily.

Chris looked up at him briefly. "Yes. That's correct," he said before again giving his attention to Andrew. "But I promise you, you'll see me anytime you want. Daddy isn't moving far away, so I can still take you to school and pick you up. When Mummy is away, you and James will stay with me, and we can have movie nights and eat loads of pizza. Would you like that?"

Andrew nodded, but tears were in his eyes. "But Andrew wants you to live here, Daddy."

"Well, he can't because Mum said so!" James snapped.

"Mum said what?"

Chris and the boys turned to see Elizabeth standing in the doorway. Rising to his feet, he pulled Andrew close and gave him a gentle pat on the head.

"You said Dad can't live here anymore, and I hate you for it!" James blurted out and turned to leave, but Chris grabbed his arm and prevented him.

As James faced his father, Chris saw that he was struggling with unshed tears visible in his eyes.

"Son, I appreciate you're upset, but you can't speak to your mother like that."

James pulled away from his father. "Well, I'm not apologising." He turned to Elizabeth. "I meant what I said. I hate you, and I'm going to make your life hell!" He stormed off, leaving both parents watching in shock.

Before they recovered, Andrew, who always imitated his older brother, stomped his foot angrily. "Me too!" he said, and he ran after James.

A sigh escaped Chris's lips as he scratched his head. "They're upset. They don't mean what they've said," he assured Elizabeth, who looked white as a sheet. "Give them a couple of days to come round."

Elizabeth nodded without speaking and stood to one side as Chris manipulated his suitcases out of the door and out of their home.

CHAPTER THREE

Mabel stood at the kitchen sink, a cup of coffee cradled in her hands, looking out the window. She appeared to be admiring the back garden, which had only just been reconstructed in preparation for summer, but she wasn't. She was lost in her thoughts. A lot had happened since that horrible morning in January last year when she woke up to find her husband gone.

His little note had been such a massive shock that she collapsed upon reading it. After the paramedics revived her, she tried to pull herself together and stay strong for the girls. She contacted family and friends in Lagos, his and hers, but none offered helpful information. Then, a week later, her younger sister called and informed her that Barry visited their uncle, who played the role of a father following their father's demise, and he'd returned the bride price.

With the return of the bride price, her marriage to Barry was officially over. They did not marry in the registry or church, so there was no long-drawn-out divorce battle. It was over, and there was talk of him planning to marry another woman. The news caused her to break down and be hospitalised for a fortnight. It had been a blessing in disguise, for it was while in the hospital that she met Pastor John Griffith. She would never forget that day because meeting him completely changed her life.

"That's the pastor from London with the megachurch. I see him on television very often," the elderly woman in the bed beside hers said.

Mabel looked up, and her eyes met John's. He stood across the ward from her, where he'd been previously talking with a young woman admitted only the day before. His appearance wasn't that of a pastor. Casually dressed in jeans, a shirt, and a leather biker jacket, he looked like a celebrity movie star. At approximately six foot three, he was a very attractive man, built like an athlete, with blond hair and blue eyes. He towered over the doctor he was talking to, and while he looked away after their eyes initially met, Mabel continued to stare. She'd never seen a more beautiful man.

"He is an excellent teacher of the word with a powerful healing ministry. He was a doctor but only for a short time before he became a full-time pastor."

Mabel turned to look at the woman in the adjacent bed and didn't inquire about the man's other attributes. There was no time to because he stopped talking to the doctor and headed towards her. She swallowed as she watched him cross the ward to her bedside, wishing she could look in a mirror and make herself a little more presentable.

"Hello. My name is John Griffith. I'm a pastor and came to pray with a member's sister who's hospitalised here. I noticed you from across the ward. Can I visit with you for a few minutes?"

That was how Mabel became acquainted with Pastor John. He chatted with her for almost half an hour, and she learnt that he was based in London with a megachurch but was in Manchester for a week as part of his plan to open a church branch there. Mabel confided in him about her marriage and her husband leaving her, something she hadn't done with her pastor or church community. She gave them the impression that her husband had travelled to Lagos to deal with a family emergency and would be away for a few months.

But she opened up to Pastor John. She thought him different from her pastor and any other pastor she knew. He loved people, and when he spoke to her, she perceived he wasn't thinking of his next appointment or waiting impatiently for the meeting to end. He was there in the moment, seeing, hearing, and speaking to her. She sensed her story was safe with him. It would not be used as a topic for his next sermon or shared with others, who would turn it into the latest church gossip. After meeting her for the first time and listening to her story, he visited her daily to talk and pray for her. After she was discharged, he visited her home and met the girls who fell in love with him on sight.

He spoke extensively about his church in London, and after he returned to London, Mabel decided that if she were going to leave Manchester, she would move to London. She believed her meeting with Pastor John not to be an accident but a divinely orchestrated event to rescue her from the depression that threatened to consume her. She was right.

Pastor John encouraged her to move to London. He thought leaving Manchester and starting afresh in London would help rid her of depression, and neither she nor the girls would have to face questions about Barry and why he wasn't around. The house was in her sole name, as Barry gifted it to her when Daisy was born, so she put it up for sale and bought a property in Hampstead, London, where Pastor John lived and where The Vine Church was situated. She wanted to be as close to him as possible, and her new house was only a short drive from his house and the church.

Not that she ever visited his residence. He came to hers, and she visited him in the office. But she stayed away from his home primarily because she didn't like his wife. She recalled their first meeting. It had been at the children's school. Pastor John had personally been involved in helping her and the girls settle into their new home, guided her in selecting a suitable Christian independent school, and even accompanied her on the girls' first day back at school. Pastor John's children went to the school, which took kids from five to eighteen, but Mabel didn't know this because he never discussed his family.

Daisy performed exceptionally well that term and was due a prize on the end-of-year prize-giving day. Pastor John was excited because the girls had only been in the school that summer term and so when Daisy invited him to come to school to watch her receive her prize, he happily obliged.

On the day, Mabel and John arrived in their own cars at about the same time, and as they walked through the car park towards the school's main entrance, he spotted his wife. She was there to witness their children receive prizes. Mabel recognised her from church. Why wouldn't she? She was the senior pastor's wife, and although she held no position or title in the church, she sat next to her husband during every service. Their seats on the altar were hard to miss, no matter how far away from the altar one sat.

Pastor John performed the introductions, and Mabel watched as his wife plastered on a smile that did not reach her eyes.

"Lovely to make your acquaintance," she said and turned to her husband. "You didn't tell me you were coming here today. The kids will be glad to have you watch them receive their prizes."

"The kids are receiving prizes?"

"Yes. All three of them." She looked up at him, smiling.

John looked thrilled. "Excellent! Let's find front-row seats then."

And just like that, Victoria Griffith hijacked her husband. She linked her arm with his and walked into the hall, leaving Mabel behind. When they sat, Victoria ensured she was sitting in between them. She monopolised Pastor John the entire time and made it impossible for Mabel to talk with him. Daisy received one prize, and Mabel was pleased as Pastor John stood up and clapped heartily for her. She saw him, grinned ear-to-ear, and waved.

Then Victoria turned to her. "Is it just one prize she's won?"

That dampened Mabel's mood, especially because Victoria's son Paul won so many prizes. Jokingly, the teacher presenting the gifts said at one point, "I think you should stay on stage, Paul Griffith, as we will call on you again."

"Yes, it's one prize."

"She's done well. John's just informed me it's her first term here. You must be proud of her."

"I am," Mabel said. "Very proud."

"John and I are very proud of our brood. They've been winning prizes consistently every year since they started school," Victoria said, and then turned to her husband, rubbing his knee to get his attention. "Haven't they, darling?"

John shrugged. "It's what they're here for: to excel."

Victoria turned to look at Mabel. "They take after their father. I chose the best man to have babies with."

Mabel watched as Victoria ostentatiously rubbed her husband's knee while speaking. It was a subtle reminder that he was hers; as if anyone would forget. Her other two children also performed well and won prizes, although not as many as the youngest. When it was time for pictures, Victoria directed the session, preventing Mabel from getting a picture with Pastor John and her daughters. But Mabel quickly rectified that by inviting him to a celebratory dinner at her home the following evening. And the girls got all the attention and pictures they'd been deprived the day before.

That meeting with Victoria left a bitter taste in her mouth, so she never attempted to visit Pastor John at home. It was irrelevant since he visited her residence upon invitation, and she had access to him at his workplace as desired. He was truly involved in their lives. He checked on her and the girls regularly, and because of him, the girls fully settled into their new church and made friends. They were handling the issue of their absent father a lot better than they would have without Pastor John's influence. She owed him so much.

Spending time with him also made her want to improve herself. He didn't pressure her to lose weight or make her think poorly of herself for lacking a degree, but his love and acceptance inspired her to improve. Ten months ago, she revamped her life, starting university and hitting the gym. She had dropped from dress size eighteen to dress size ten and looked younger, more beautiful, and vibrant.

Pastor John held her hand every step of the way, and the desire for his applause kept her motivated on both her academic and weight loss journeys. Feeling like there was nothing she could not accomplish, three months ago, she launched her clothing business, *Ara*, which manufactured and sold African dresses.

The girls, too, flourished under his constant praise. He was their biggest supporter, offering encouragement and a listening ear as they shared their school worries and problems, trusting in his positive advice. Little Daisy, who had been shy and unsure of herself, became more confident as he admired her and told her she was beautiful and smart. Every morning and night before bed, Daisy religiously chanted the powerful Bible affirmations he'd written for her.

The previous time he visited, he saw the back garden remained overgrown as it was when she and the girls arrived the preceding year. He commented that the girls needed the space to play as summer was approaching, and the following day, he sent her to the gardening firm that handled the church's gardens, and they transformed her garden at a discounted price. She smiled as she looked at the garden, which had been completed earlier today. Pastor John was an amazing man, and his presence meant she hadn't missed Barry's absence. Mabel was lost in thought, so Tracy's entrance to the kitchen went unnoticed.

"Mum?" Tracy spoke just a little above a whisper, but when it became obvious that Mabel hadn't heard her, she raised her voice. "Mum!"

Mabel turned around sharply to look at Tracy. "Yes, dear, what is it?"

Tracy didn't respond. Instead, she moved closer and put her hand on Mabel's shoulder, looking into her eyes as she did.

"Mum, are you okay?" she asked, and Mabel noticed the concern on her young teenager's face.

She smiled, put her cup on the kitchen table, and embraced Tracy. Her precious daughter had been a companion and pillar of strength for the last year. Following Barry's departure, the teen quickly matured.

Mabel watched with pride as she took charge of her younger sisters, ensuring they were well taken care of and did not disturb their mother unless necessary. Mabel sometimes wondered what she would have done without her.

"Yes, dear. Mum is fine. Thank you for asking, and acting so grown up, and taking good care of Mum."

Tracy pulled back and studied at her mother thoughtfully. "Seriously, Mum, are you okay?"

"Yes, I am, Mum," Mabel teased, and a chuckle escaped Tracy's lips. "So what did you want?" She picked up her cup again and sipped her drink.

"Pastor's on the phone. The house phone. He wants to talk to you."

"Oh, he is?" She put down her cup and walked briskly out of the kitchen.

When she entered the living room, Daisy was on the phone talking to Pastor John, and an impatient Stacy was near, looking like she would grab the phone out of Daisy's hand in a minute. As Mabel approached, she turned to her.

"Mum, Daisy won't let me talk to Pastor," she complained.

"You already spoke to him, Stacy. Stop being silly," Tracy chided.

Stacy pouted. "I didn't get to tell him about my new dress from *Ara*.

Tracy rolled her eyes. "He'll see you in church tomorrow wearing the dress, and you can tell him all about it."

"But that's not fair. Daisy's telling him about her dress."

"Enough, Stacy," Mabel intervened, stroking Stacy's cheek lovingly. "Tracy's right. Pastor will see you in your new dress from *Ara* tomorrow."

Mabel sat in the armchair closest to Daisy and pried the phone from her hand, whispering as she did, "Say goodnight to Pastor."

"I have to go now, Pastor. But I'll see you tomorrow, and you can tell me what you think of my dress."

"I'm sure you'll look even more beautiful than Cinderella, Daisy," Pastor John said, and Daisy giggled.

"Goodnight, Pastor. I love you."

"Goodnight, Daisy. I love you, too. The Lord watch over you and keep you."

"Amen," Daisy muttered and passed the phone to her mother.

"Good evening, Pastor John," Mabel greeted beaming.

"Mabel! Good evening. How are you?"

"As well as can be expected."

"Good. I'm glad to hear it. I understand that the gardeners finished the work on your garden today?"

Mabel's smile widened at the mention of her new garden. "Yes, they did. It's beautiful."

"So, you like it?"

"Like it? I love it. They did a brilliant job."

"That's what I like to hear when I refer someone to do a job. Not that I had any doubts about their ability to deliver on their promise. They've worked for the church for many years and in my home, so I have the utmost faith in them. However, it's always good to have feedback that aligns with my thoughts. So, how are you preparing for church tomorrow?"

"I'm ready. The girls have their clothes laid out, we've had our Bible study in spiritual preparation, and we're going to have dinner in a little while and be off to bed."

"Excellent. I'm looking forward to seeing you all tomorrow. Have you given any thought to our last conversation?"

He wanted her to become part of the helps ministry within the church as he believed that she had much to offer God's people and was ready to begin active service in God's vineyard again. But a part of her sensed that if she became active, she would be viewed as a mature believer, no longer needing the support of Pastor John, and being required to offer the same support to others. Mabel wasn't ready for her contact with him to diminish, but how did she tell him without sounding selfish?

"I have," she murmured.

"And?"

"I don't think I'm ready to get involved to the point where people learn my story."

Pastor John was quiet for a while as he reflected on her response. No one in The Vine Church knew Mabel's story. They probably assumed her husband lived abroad. He appreciated that working closely with others in serving the Lord may expose her. He saw no problems. The man was a sinner and an irresponsible husband and father. Mabel shouldn't have to be criticised for that. But humans were humans, and as much as he tried to teach the right values at church, there were people who would gossip if they learned she was divorced.

"Okay, Mabel. Take your time."

A triumphant smile crossed Mabel's lips. "Thank you, Pastor John. Goodnight."

Mabel looked at the phone in her hand for a moment before putting it down. He was such a dear man, Pastor John. She envied his wife and children. They didn't recognise how lucky they were. She would give an arm to have a man like that as her husband and the father of her girls.

"Mum, I'm hungry!"

Mabel looked up at Stacy as she dragged herself out of her reverie and stood to her feet,

"It's dinner time," she announced. "Stacy, you and Daisy set the table. Tracy, come and help me in the kitchen."

CHAPTER FOUR

After dinner, John returned to his study and locked himself in, intending to make a few calls to check on some church members and then review his sermon notes. He made the calls and was reviewing his notes when his phone rang. With a sigh, he answered it.

"Hello, this is Pastor John."

The person at the other end of the line began to cry. John furrowed his brows. He knew it was a female. No doubt a member of his congregation.

"Good evening, Pastor." The caller greeted him once the wailing died down. "It's me, Georgieta."

He frowned, wondering what the issue was again. Georgieta was a beautiful young lady in her early twenties. She was from Sierra Leone and recently returned to the UK, her country of birth, seeking greener pastures after living in Sierra Leone for two decades. She lived with a distant relative, Mariatu, who was a long-standing member of The Vine Church and the assistant worship leader.

Georgieta was struggling financially as she was yet to secure full-time work. To ease her burden on Mariatu, a month ago, he offered Mariatu a hundred pounds weekly to enable Georgieta to live peacefully in her home until she found steady work and got her own place. His private secretary, Liam, assured him that Mariatu received the weekly payments. But yesterday, Georgieta called with some complaints which he refused to listen to, preferring Mariatu to be present. He called Mariatu and asked her to attend a meeting with Georgieta in his office after church on Sunday so he might address the issue and resolve it.

"Ah, Georgieta, yes. What's the matter? You sound very upset. Are you okay?"

"No, Pastor, I'm not. Mariatu is mad at me. She says I came to see you and told you negative things about her to make her look bad before you, and she's been giving me grief since yesterday."

"But you're still in her house? She hasn't thrown you out?"

"She hasn't thrown me out, Pastor. But she's asked me to pack up my things because after meeting you tomorrow, I won't be returning to her house." Once again, she broke down in tears.

"I wouldn't worry about tomorrow, Georgieta. Tomorrow's not here yet. You both come to my office after church for that meeting, and I'll try to resolve the issue. If it can't be resolved, I'll find you another place to live. You won't be stranded or homeless."

"Okay, Pastor. Thank you."

"You're welcome, Georgieta."

He ended the call, and the door opened, and Victoria peered in.

He looked up with a frown as he placed the phone on the desk beside his laptop. Victoria knew he didn't like to be disturbed when he disappeared into his study on a Saturday night.

"Pastor Ben is here to see you," she announced before his inquiry regarding the interruption.

His frown deepened. "Pastor Ben?"

Pastor Benjamin Nkosi was a black South African pastor who recently joined The Vine Church as a junior pastor. He was not only a junior pastor but was still on year-long probation, which meant specific assignments were not yet committed to his hands, and he was still being observed.

"What does he want?" John asked, still surprised. There was no meeting scheduled with the young man. Besides, Pastor Ben had never visited his house. The few times they had met, it had been in the office.

Victoria shrugged and grinned playfully. "How should I know?"

"Just send him in!" John snapped irritably. He was not in the mood for Victoria's playful moments.

He pushed back his beautifully upholstered leather swivel chair and rose as Pastor Ben entered his home office. Victoria shut the door quietly, leaving both men alone.

"Good evening, Pastor Ben." John reached out and shook hands with the younger man, who looked uncomfortable and avoided eye contact. "I understand that you want to see me." He waved to the pair of burgundy handcrafted leather chairs on the other side of the desk and settled himself again in his high-backed leather swivel chair.

"Good evening, Pastor John." Ben looked up at him but avoided meeting his gaze. "Thank you for seeing me, and I apologise for disrupting your evening. I realise you're preparing for tomorrow's service."

John shrugged, leaning back in his chair and observing the man before him. "No need to apologise, Ben. You have something important to say, or you wouldn't be here. Let's hear it."

Just then, John's mobile phone, lying on the desk between him and Pastor Ben, rang. Glancing at the screen, Pastor Ben saw it was Mariatu, and he jumped to his feet.

"Please don't answer any call from Mariatu. Hear me out first."

John frowned as he reached for his phone. "Pastor Ben, please calm down and sit down. Mariatu is calling because I asked her to see me after church tomorrow."

Now, Pastor Ben looked confused. "You know she's pregnant?" he asked, sitting down.

John's hand froze over the mobile phone. What did Pastor Ben mean? Mariatu was a single woman, vibrant, serving the Lord. Granted, she was approaching forty and often frustrated about her lack of ability to find a husband

and what she described as her fading beauty. Reasons, he suspected, made her antagonistic toward the much younger, beautiful Georgieta.

"Mariatu is pregnant?" John asked, pushing away the phone that had stopped ringing and giving Pastor Ben his full attention. "And how do you know this, Pastor Ben?"

John had to ask. The last time he saw Mariatu, a few days ago, at the midweek Bible study meeting, she led worship and didn't look pregnant. He was a pastor who hated gossip, so if she confided in Pastor Ben and he was here to betray that confidence, instead of encouraging her to come forward herself, he would give him a serious talking to.

"I am responsible." Pastor Ben's voice dropped so low that John thought he had misheard him.

"What was that?"

"I am responsible for Sister Mariatu's pregnancy."

John let out a deep sigh and then quickly processed the news. As a pastor for over two decades, he'd witnessed and heard everything.

"Pastor Ben, I think the first thing is not to use the title sister when discussing Mariatu. To claim responsibility for her pregnancy while simultaneously calling her your sister seems a bit too contradictory and hypocritical, don't you think?"

"You're right, Pastor John."

"Good. Now tell me what's going on."

Pastor Ben looked up but avoided meeting John's gaze. "We've been having an affair for a few months. At first, I told myself it was because my wife had yet to come from South Africa to join me. But when she came, she was already in the second trimester of her pregnancy and losing interest in sex."

Pastor Ben was married to a woman from his hometown, and the marriage was blessed with a four-year-old daughter. His wife was currently pregnant with their second child. John was initially uncomfortable with Pastor Ben coming from South Africa without his wife, Gloria. But the pregnancy made her ill and unable to fly at the time, and he thought that as they would only be parted a couple of months, no damage would be done. He thought wrong.

"So you continued your affair with Mariatu, and now she's pregnant?"

Pastor Ben nodded. "Yes, Pastor John."

John pushed his chair away from his desk and sat with his left ankle on his right knee. "So, why did you choose to come and see me tonight?"

Pastor Ben shifted uncomfortably in his seat. "Well, I only just found out from Mariatu. She asked me to meet her at home, where she broke the news. I can't tell my wife; she will have our baby any day. There's no telling how that kind of news will affect her in the last days of her pregnancy. Mariatu is demanding that I officially introduce myself to her family and introduce her to mine before the baby is born so it will be accepted. That's not something I can do behind my wife's back."

"Unlike sneaking around to Mariatu's house and getting into her bed!"

"Yes, Pastor John."

"You still haven't told me why you came to me. Yes, Mariatu wants recognition, but why is this relevant to me?"

"She threatened to call you and tell you I'd been sleeping with her if I didn't comply with her demands."

"Ah. I see. Now, that makes sense."

Once again, Pastor Ben looked down at his hands. The phone began to ring again. It was Mariatu, and John answered it and put it on speaker.

"Good evening, Mariatu."

"Good evening, Pastor John."

"I have put you on speaker because I have Pastor Ben in my office." He waited for the words to sink in.

"Yes, Pastor."

John folded his arms across his broad chest. "I'm sure you know why he is in my office." He didn't wait for a response. "This is what's going to happen. I have asked for a meeting with you and Georgieta after service tomorrow. Are you aware?"

"Yes, Pastor. She told me."

"Good. I will meet with you and Georgieta first. Following the resolution of that issue, Georgieta will leave, and Pastor Ben will join us to discuss the matter he's brought to my attention. You will both continue with your duties during tomorrow's service because I do not want the church agog with gossip before or during the service. Following our talk, I will decide on steps to correct this wrong."

"Yes, Pastor," Mariatu said in a low voice. "Good night."

"Good night." John ended the call, dropped his feet, and pushed his chair closer to his desk. He looked up at Pastor Ben. "Have I made myself clear?"

Pastor Ben nodded vigorously, rising to his feet. "Yes, Pastor John. Tomorrow in your office after service. Thank you. Good night." He hurried towards the door.

"Good night," John mumbled as the door opened and Pastor Ben exited hastily.

***

As John rose and approached the pulpit, he briefly considered the events of yesterday evening. The choir was still singing a beautiful worship song, and all around him, pastors and congregants alike lifted their hands in worship, but he was too grieved in his spirit to worship. He did not feel the presence of God as he stood on the elevated circular-shaped altar, microphone in hand and surveyed the vast auditorium with thousands lifting hands in worship and singing with the choir as they prepared to receive the word. Not for the first time did he wonder if The Vine Church was about to experience a major scandal or disintegration that he had observed in other churches.

How had his junior pastor, a man with a pregnant wife, become sexually involved with the assistant worship leader? How would the issue impact the church? There was no way it could be kept hidden. Ben's wife would have to be told. How would she handle it? Georgieta lived with Mariatu and must suspect something. She might discuss her observations with others within or outside the church. Whichever way, he saw a scandal coming. If the press learned of this, he envisioned the headlines: Pastor impregnates worship leader at The Vine Church. It would affect the church's activities, particularly the fortnightly evangelism across all London boroughs.

As he flipped through his sermon notes, half-heartedly following the worship song, his thoughts drifted back to the preceding year when a dear friend suffered a scandal that ruined his church and his life, causing him to take his own life as he was overwhelmed by shame. Pastor Mark Evans became his friend while they were at university; afterwards, Mark relocated to America and established a church. As great friends, they did ministry together, inviting each other to speak and sometimes travelling together to Africa to preach in the nooks and crannies of the cities in East and West Africa. Mark loved the Lord, but his church scandal destroyed him.

John remembered the call he received from Mark as if it were yesterday. It had been their last conversation. As he picked up the call, he perceived something was wrong, and it was evident in Mark's weak, lacklustre greeting. The vibrant Pastor Mark was missing.

"Hey, Mark. Is everything okay? How's Christine?"

Mark laughed drily. "She's left me."

John froze to the spot because Mark and Christine had been married for fifteen years with two beautiful daughters. As far as he was aware, they were a happy family. Every time he preached in their church, he stayed in their home, and there was nothing to indicate they were anything but joyful and content.

"What's going on, Mark?" he asked.

"It's a long story."

"I've got time, Mark. Tell me."

Mark Evans sighed. "Things are a mess just now, John. It's not just my family. It's the entire church. Everything's a mess. A scandal is brewing, and it will be huge. I am uncertain about how to survive it or continue ministry afterwards."

"Don't say that, Mark. We'll pray together, and God will show us a way around whatever it is."

Mark laughed. "Perhaps," he said but sounded doubtful, almost hopeless. Mark never sounded hopeless, and that should have been John's first clue that he was contemplating taking his life.

"Tell me what's going on," he encouraged.

"About a year ago, a lady, Mia, joined the church from the LGBT community."

"I remember Mia," John said. When Mia joined the church, he was visiting America to preach for Mark.

John remembered how she testified that Jesus led her away from the gay lifestyle, having been a lesbian for more than ten years. While John was greatly moved by her testimony, he believed she should undergo deliverance before being accepted into the church family. He mentioned it to Mark, but Mark thought a deliverance was unnecessary since she had been led to Christ and was born again.

"After Mia joined the church, a lot happened. Mia has now left the church and lives with Olivia. Olivia is the wife of Christine's younger brother, the worship leader. I understand that both women were acquainted before Mia joined the church and had sex on one occasion. They're now openly in a relationship, and Olivia has left her husband and two small children. Mia was also involved with my assistant pastor, Pastor Elijah, and Mia may or may not have been involved with Christine. It's not clear if there was a threesome involving Mia, Pastor Elijah and Christine. But Christine has been involved with Pastor Elijah for months and is pregnant by him. They're moving away to Florida to start a church."

John remained silent for a long time, unsure what to say to his friend of many years. The following day, he received a call that Mark Evans had died from a drug overdose. Mark chose to end his life rather than face the scandal. And the scandal came, and it was nasty. The press tore the church to shreds, and it shut down almost immediately, with members distancing themselves hastily.

He lifted his hand, signalling the choir that it was time to end the singing. He cleared his throat.

"Technical team, this isn't the message for the day, and I don't want it recorded, so shut down all recording devices, audio and visual. Brethren, turn to 2 Chronicles 7:14-16. I am reading from the King James Version. It says, if my people, which are called by my name, shall humble themselves, and pray, and seek my face, and turn from their wicked ways; then will I hear from heaven, and will forgive their sin, and will heal their land.

"This is a day for repentance, people of God. God is calling each of us to turn from our wicked ways, wicked ways of fornication and adultery, wicked ways of covetousness and drunkenness. Let us repent from the evil we do when we think no one watches us, for God sees even our secret thoughts. Let us repent of a lying tongue, a heart that devises wickedness and feet that are swift to run to mischief. Some of us must come to the altar now and rededicate our lives to God."

John led the congregation in repentance before the Lord for the next half-hour. The choir sang, "For You are glorious and worthy to be praised, the Lamb upon the throne. And unto You, we lift our voice in praise, the Lamb upon the throne!"

Wailing mixed with the song pervaded the atmosphere as the people turned from their wrongdoings.

CHAPTER FIVE

"Hello, Liam." A smile touched Victoria's lips as she entered the reception area leading to John's office.

The room was brightly lit and relaxing, with large windows that let in a generous amount of natural light, comfortable visitor chairs, and a wide-screen television on the wall. A small group of people sat together, their eyes fixed intently on the television as it played an old message from a previous Sunday, the familiar tones drawing them into a shared moment of nostalgia and reflection.

"Hello, Victoria." From behind his desk, Liam beamed at her, springing to attention. "May I say that you look very lovely today? Your new hairstyle suits you."

Victoria was a vision in a white two-piece skirt suit with faux feather trimmings on the hem of the sleeves and skirt. Her sliver stiletto sandals, clutch purse and elegant fascinator hat with its ostrich feathers were the perfect ensembles. She cut her hair into a chic bob with bangs the day before, perfectly complementing her attire. John had not noticed. But what was new?

"Thank you, Liam. What a kind thing to say." She beamed back at him, her smile mirroring his warmth. "Is it okay to go in?"

"It's always okay for you to go in, Victoria. It's called spouse privilege."

Her smile expressed her thanks as she walked towards the oak door at the far end of the room, pushing it open and going inside. No matter how often she visited, Victoria always found John's office a little too formal. It was a cold space, with its white walls and flooring. In the centre of the room sat John's large, white curved desk, and with its white high-backed leather swivel chair, there were a couple of white leather armchairs on the other side of the desk and a white leather Chesterfield sofa in the corner. Perhaps the only warmth in the room emanated from the multicoloured books on the white shelves behind the desk.

John stood in the middle of the room, away from his desk, surrounded by a woman and three young girls. Victoria recognised Mabel instantly. Why wouldn't she? The woman was never far away from her husband! They all looked beautiful in African-style clothes. Mabel wore an Asoke kaftan dress and matching headpiece, and her daughters wore A-line skater dresses and fascinators, all in matching Asoke fabric.

"Ah, Victoria, you're here. Would you please take a picture of me with Mabel and the girls?"

"Of course," Victoria stepped further into the office, placed her clutch purse and Bible on the desk and took the phone Mabel was extending in her direction. "Your shoelaces are undone, John," she pointed out as she stood in position, ready to take a shot.

"Oh, are they?" John looked down at his feet.

"I'll help you out." Mabel knelt down and hurriedly tied the shoelaces.

Victoria watched the scene before her with a raised brow.

"That's better, now," John said, oblivious to Victoria's reaction. "Thank you, Mabel."

She flashed him a smile. "You're welcome, Pastor John."

"Everyone say cheese!" Daisy shouted, bringing everyone's attention back to the photo that was about to be taken.

Everyone laughed—everyone except Victoria, who tried to keep a small smile on her face as she took the photos and handed the phone back to Mabel.

"Thank you." Mabel grinned like the Cheshire Cat. She asked her daughters, "What do you say to the nice lady for taking the pictures?"

"Thank you!" All three girls chorused.

Victoria smiled. "You're welcome." She picked up her clutch bag and Bible and stood to one side. Once it became clear that she was not about to talk to her husband in front of an audience, Mabel turned to John.

"We'll be leaving now, Pastor John. Thank you for indulging the girls' request for a photo."

"Thank you for taking a picture with us, Pastor," Stacy said.

"I was unable to resist; you all look beautiful in your African dresses."

"My dress is the prettiest." Pastor John laughed as Daisy spun around.

"No, it's not. Mine is. Isn't it, Pastor John?" Stacy asked.

"Will you two stop already?" Tracy sounded irritated. "Your dresses are the same. All our dresses are from *Ara*."

"Everyone looks beautiful in their dresses," John declared. "Tracy is beautiful, Stacy is beautiful, Daisy is beautiful, even Mummy is beautiful. *Ara* makes the prettiest dresses."

Mabel grinned. "Thank you, Pastor John, for the compliments. The girls can't get enough of hearing you tell them how beautiful they look."

"I'll never get tired of saying it." John took the bottle of anointing oil from his desk and anointed each girl. As he did, he declared, "The Lord bless you and keep you and make His face shine on you and be gracious to you."

Victoria stepped out of the way and watched Mabel herd her brood out of the office. As she left, Pastor Tom appeared in the open doorway and looked in to speak to John, pausing as he saw Victoria. At The Vine Church, Pastor Tom served as vice president and was John's right-hand man.

"Hello, Victoria. I was going to say earlier that you look stunning today. Your new hairstyle suits you." He turned to John. "She does look stunning, doesn't she?"

John turned to look at Victoria as if he were seeing her for the first time. He frowned as he took in her white skirt suit, stilettos, and fascinator. His frown deepened as he noticed the chic bob hairstyle. He wondered when she had cut her hair.

"Yes, she looks stunning," he said almost absentmindedly.

"I'm going home with Blossom and the kids to have lunch," Pastor Tom announced. "I'll be back in an hour or two."

"Sure," John said. "See you later."

As Pastor Tom shut the door behind him, Victoria turned to John. "I'm leaving now with the kids," she informed him. "Would you like me to bring you some lunch?"

He shook his head as he returned to his desk and sat in his chair. "I have a sandwich and some fruit in the fridge. I'll be fine. You go home and get some rest."

"Fine. See you later." Victoria turned and walked towards the door.

As she walked toward her car, parked in front of the church office building, she searched for her children. In the distance, she saw Paul and the housekeeper Lindsay, a plump middle-aged woman, on the church's steps greeting a few parishioners. John Jr. would be rounding up with the ushering team. She had seen Rebekah speaking with a friend before entering the church office, but now she was nowhere to be found. She sighed as she pulled out her phone to send a text message asking her to come to the car.

"Why did John lead the church to repentance and ask the media team not to record it? What's going on?"

Victoria looked up from texting Rebekah as her sister-in-law, Elizabeth, joined her in front of the car. As always, Elizabeth looked dazzling in a red silk cape dress accentuating her figure. It was cinched at the waist, and the asymmetrical cape fell over her right shoulder. Her long blond hair was held back in a chignon, and she wore a red fascinator with netting trimming styled into a bow on the side. Designer suede pumps and a clutch bag completed her attire.

"I'm just as lost as you are. John doesn't discuss church matters with me."

Elizabeth wrinkled her nose. "That's a shame. It would have been nice to know. I'm sure something's happened. Knowing John, he wouldn't lead the church to repent unless something unexpected happened. I'm curious if this involves Chris and me."

As Elizabeth said the words, she regretted them. John wouldn't bring her marital issues to church. But as she and Barry became lovers while Chris lived in the matrimonial home, she wondered if he'd been referring to her when he talked about turning from wicked ways of adultery. She was being silly. John knew nothing about Barry. He knew about her problems with Chris, but that did not constitute adultery. Her affair with Barry did constitute adultery, but she would make her peace with God eventually before she saw Him. While she wasn't as crazy in love with Jesus as John was, she didn't want to spend eternity in hell.

"You and Chris?" Victoria looked surprised. "Why would it have anything to do with you and Chris? Where is he anyway?" Victoria turned around as if trying to catch a glimpse of Chris David-West.

"He moved out last night." Elizabeth gave a nonchalant shrug. "He's probably not in church today. I thought John told you."

"If you thought so, you still haven't understood your brother. He did mention he was going over to yours, but he doesn't talk about his discussions with people, and I have learnt not to ask. In the early days of our marriage, I did and was reprimanded. He asked how it concerned our family."

Elizabeth let out a humourless laugh. "Yes. That sounds like John. I can picture him asking how it's your business. I could never have married him." She shuddered.

Victoria poked her playfully and laughed. "That's why he's your brother."

"Yes. It's better that way." Elizabeth said. "I still wish I knew what was going on, though."

Victoria rolled her eyes. She had learnt to avoid church gossip. John detested it, and when she was involved, he was less lenient with her.

"Here comes Audrey. She'll know what's going on," Elizabeth said.

Victoria stifled a groan. This was not happening. She glanced around the church premises and wished her children would finish so she might leave.

"Hello, Victoria. Elizabeth. How lovely to see you two. How are you ladies doing?" Audrey greeted as she approached. "You both look well, as always."

Audrey Campbell appeared stylish and younger than her sixty years in a green silk suit featuring wide-leg trousers and a long double-breasted jacket that reached her ankles. Her intricately braided hair was elegantly coiled into a graceful bun atop her head, adding an air of sophistication to her appearance. She was a tall, slender, Togolese woman married to a white British man, and the women's leader at The Vine Church.

Victoria initially resented her appointment, thinking that as the senior pastor's wife, she should have that position, but she now understood why John appointed Audrey as leader of the women. The church had grown in membership following her appointment. She understood how to draw women into the church, and they subsequently brought in their husbands, children, and grandchildren.

Victoria would never have been able to do what Audrey did, being an introverted person. Audrey was an extroverted, charismatic leader. It was a shame, though, that she had failed to persuade her husband to become a committed church member. He was content to attend services only during Christmas and Easter. She was just as ineffective with her three sons; the oldest was in prison for carrying a knife, the middle son, at twenty-one, had fathered multiple children with multiple women, and the youngest constantly had brushes with the law. Her other problem was that she loved gossip.

Victoria smiled at her. "Thank you, Audrey. You always say such nice things. How are you?"

"I am as well as can be and very busy with arrangements for the cookout on Easter Monday."

"Ah. The cookout. I heard the women set up a committee and are planning a big party for the community," Elizabeth said.

"Yes, indeed. Pastor John is excited about it. He says it's a way to reach out to the community and bring the lost to Christ." A certain something caught her attention, causing her to pause and sigh. "Why does she take her children to see Pastor John every Sunday?"

Victoria looked at Audrey and followed her gaze in time to see Freya Thomson leaving the church office with her six-month-old twins, Ethan and Ella, in her arms. Freya was a single woman in her early forties who had never married. Last year, she caused a sensation in the church when she became pregnant. After speaking with her, John informed the church that she had become pregnant through IVF. He said that while it was not something he would encourage any single person to do, he understood Freya's motivation, and her actions would not take her to hell.

The church rallied around her, but many still gossiped about her. In his characteristic manner, John became involved with Freya, acting as a substitute father for the twins, ensuring they lacked nothing. He shut down anyone who tried to discuss Freya and her actions. As for corrective measures, he was very clear that none were meted out because Freya was not in a position of authority within the church, and bringing up the children without a father was sufficient retribution.

"Why else?" Elizabeth shrugged. "She wants him to pray over them."

Audrey grimaced. "Ugh. Occasionally is fine. But every single Sunday? How many problems do they have?"

"John's not complaining," Victoria said, hoping that would end the matter.

Audrey rolled her eyes. "It's members like her who give the pastor a headache."

"Hello, ladies."

"Hello, Freya," Victoria and Elizabeth chorused.

"Ella and Ethan look well," Audrey commented. "They are growing every day."

Freya grinned, glancing down adorningly at the boisterous twins in her arms. "Yes, they are," she agreed.

"Their well-being always brings me joy," Victoria said.

"Thank you so much, Victoria." Freya's expression shifted from a smile to a frown as Ella's playful mood changed to crying. "Oh dear. That's my cue to head home. Bye, everyone."

"Bye, Freya!" Victoria and Elizabeth called out to her retreating figure.

"Freya's always been a little too carnal for my liking," Audrey muttered as they watched her go. "An unmarried woman in the church having children! It would never happen in my day as a young Christian woman. She claims IVF, but a secret lover is entirely possible, given her personality. Nevertheless, what's done in darkness shall always come to light!"

Audrey hurried away. A little perplexed, Elizabeth watched her go, then glanced at Victoria; both women were soon shaking with laughter.

"Ah, good old Audrey!" Laughter accompanied Elizabeth's words. "She can criticise Freya despite her children's shortcomings."

***

"Georgieta tells me she's been having a challenging time living in your home, and yesterday, she called to inform me that you've asked her to move out. Is that correct?" John looked from Mariatu to Georgieta.

"Yes, Pastor." Mariatu appeared downcast. It was unbelievable that she was the same person who'd asked Georgieta to move out.

"Georgieta, now that Mariatu is present, please tell me the issue."

"Pastor, before I came from Sierra Leonne, it was agreed that I would stay at Mariatu's house. I was told that life in London is tough, and people pay many bills, so I promised her that I would not be a burden and that as I worked, I would support her with the bills. To show I meant what I was saying, I asked her what local foods from Sierra Leone she desired me to bring. When she offered to send me money for the items, I declined. It cost quite a bit to buy the items, and as such, I arrived with little money. The morning after I arrived, Mariatu said she was going shopping for groceries and demanded a hundred pounds from me.

"Pastor John, I was shocked. A hundred pounds? I didn't have that kind of money anywhere. Where would I get it from? I had only just returned to the UK after many years of living in Sierra Leone and had yet to secure work. I offered to give her twenty pounds, which she collected. Pastor, it was all the money left on me. An old friend offered me a cleaning job the following week, but I had no idea how I would get to the job. Then I came to church, and you took an interest in me and gave me a hundred pounds to tide me over until I began working. Once I got home, I gave Mariatu eighty pounds and kept twenty pounds, which I believed would be sufficient for my transportation to work until I was paid."

John sighed and ran a hand through his hair. He looked at Mariatu, who looked away. "Is this true, Mariatu?"

Mariatu nodded, unable to speak. John sighed again.

What was wrong with some people?

God had blessed Mariatu. Her house was fully paid off, and she worked as a midwife, earning a good salary while engaging in multiple side hustles and putting her money into several investments so she wasn't in need. Georgieta, conversely, struggled greatly, and the thought that Mariatu took money from her, given her unstable finances, made him physically ill.

"Georgieta, carry on."

"Thank you, Pastor." Georgieta's smile displayed a charming gap in her teeth. "I've been in Mariatu's house for three months Pastor, and I must confess, it's been hell. I always try my best to please her, yet it's not enough. When I get up in the morning to clean the house, she yells at me about the vacuum cleaner noise. While I sweep with a brush and dustpan, she switches off the lights, claiming I'm increasing her electricity costs.

"As I wash dishes, she criticises my water consumption, claiming it increases her bill. I give her forty pounds weekly from my on-and-off cleaning jobs, but I have no peace. I'm afraid to switch on my bedroom light because she'll accuse me of increasing the electricity bill. She forbade me from charging my laptop, and I hide to charge my phone. My nighttime bathroom trips are done in darkness to avoid waking her and raising the electricity bill."

"You give her forty pounds weekly?" John frowned. He offered Mariatu a hundred pounds weekly because he thought Georgieta lacked the means to give her any money.

"Yes, Pastor, every week, unfailingly. If she doesn't have the money by the end of the week, I'll hear about the UK's high cost of living."

"What about the money I've been giving you, Mariatu? Am I to believe that you collect a hundred pounds from me weekly for Georgieta's bills and still collect forty pounds from her?"

Georgieta gasped, looking from John to Mariatu. "Have you been giving her money because of me, Pastor?"

John was too speechless to answer. He stared at Mariatu, who lowered her head in shame.

"You need to repent, Mariatu," was his only comment before he turned to Georgieta. "Did you bring your bags with you?"

"Yes, I did, Pastor. She insisted that I do."

John nodded. He pressed the buzzer on his desk, and a moment later, the door opened, and his private secretary walked in. "Liam, does my Edgware property have any available rooms?"

"Yes, Pastor. There is a room available."

"Georgieta will be there until further notice. I will cover the rent." He turned away from Liam to Georgieta, who was beaming ear-to-ear.

"Oh, Pastor John, you truly are a man of God. Thank you so much. I am grateful. God bless you real good."

John laughed as he rose to his feet. "Amen. And you are welcome, Georgieta. In this kingdom, we are blessed to be a blessing. You go with Liam, and I will see you when you have settled into your new place."

As Georgieta rose and walked towards the door, he asked Liam, "Is Pastor Ben out there?"

"Yes, Pastor John, he is," Liam confirmed.

"Send him in."

CHAPTER SIX

"Thank you, Lindsay."

Victoria smiled at the housekeeper as she handed her the picnic basket and climbed the sweeping carpeted stairs to her bedroom. She crossed the spacious and tranquil bedroom into her feminine dressing room, tossing her Burberry cross-body bag on the chest of drawers and kicking off her square-toe Mary Jane flat shoes.

Clad in a long-sleeved denim jumpsuit with wide legs, she approached the full-length mirror, gazing at her reflection and taking several deep, cleansing breaths.

"Relax, Victoria. Don't let her provoke you. That's her intention. Don't let her succeed." Eyes closed, Victoria sought relaxation, thankful for the quiet peace of her bedroom. However, not for long.

John Jr., with Paul alongside, sprinted through the bedroom and into the dressing room, while Rebekah trailed behind more slowly.

"Mum, Paul is into wizardry, and I caught Rebekah taking her clothes off for a man on a video call."

"Mum, he's lying!" Rebekah's face turned red as she screamed.

"Mum, John's not lying," Paul said. "I saw Rebekah taking off her clothes too. And a man was on the video call talking to her."

"Will you all be quiet!" Victoria opened her eyes and momentarily looked away from the mirror to glare at her brood. "What's going on? Why are you so noisy?"

There was silence in the room, and Victoria looked from one child to the other for a while, saying nothing. Finally, her gaze rested on Rebekah.

"Rebekah, you're the oldest. Tell me, what's going on?"

"John Jr. barged into my bedroom while I was undressing. He didn't have the decency to knock."

Victoria turned to her oldest son. "John Jr., you can't do that. I have told you countless times to knock before entering Rebekah's room. She is a young lady and may be in a state of undress."

John Jr.'s eyes sparkled with amusement. "Which she was, Mum, with some man on a video call watching her."

"He's lying, Mum!"

"No, he's not! I was there. I saw everything," Paul said.

"Stay out of this, Paul," Victoria said and looked at John Jr. with displeasure. "Why is Paul here?"

"Because he has a wizard's wand you and Dad are unaware of, and he's been learning sorcery online."

With a sigh, Victoria sat on the vanity stool before her legs buckled. If John came in and heard all this, she and the kids would be in much trouble. He would blame her for not watching them as she should. He made her a stay-at-home mum and paid her handsomely for it each month so she could be on hand to guide their children in the ways of the Lord, but from all indications, she appeared to be failing in her duty.

"What's wrong with you all? If your dad hears about this, your guess is as good as mine: most of your privileges will be removed."

"I didn't do anything," John Jr. protested.

"Me neither," Rebekah mumbled.

"Be quiet, young lady. Don't say another word, or I will call your father immediately and report your misbehaviour!" She stood and scowled at Rebekah. "John Jr. would not make that sort of thing up. I don't know what you're up to, but I have told you repeatedly that I don't have to; the Lord sees all and will expose it when the time is right. Take your brother's discovery as a warning; stop what you're doing before things get worse. I didn't raise you to sin and cover it up. Admitting fault and requesting God's mercy is the first indication of repentance for misdeeds. Denying wrongdoing before God will only worsen the situation."

"I was naughty, Mummy. Don't tell Daddy. I'm sorry, I won't do it again," Paul said.

Victoria smiled at her youngest and pulled him to her, ruffling his hair. "Learn a lesson from Paul, Rebekah. A broken and contrite heart, God never despises, but when we add sin to sin by lying instead of repenting, then God's wrath and judgement await us."

Rebekah looked down at her sock-clad feet. "I'm sorry, Mum."

"Good. I need you to go to your bedroom and repent before the Lord. You understand when you're behaving correctly and when you're not. Ask God for mercy and forgiveness, and we'll have a conversation before bedtime." Victoria looked at Paul. "And that goes for you too, little man."

As all three children walked out of her bedroom, she called out after them, "I'm going to need to see your notes from the service after dinner."

With a sigh, she dropped back onto the vanity stool. "Help me, Lord," she prayed.

Was it possible for this day to get any worse? she wondered. First, Mabel audaciously tied John's shoelaces, not minding that his wife was present. Her relationship with the man lacked boundaries. That was not all. Once she got home, she packed a picnic basket and went back to the church, intending to spend an hour in the office with John as he enjoyed a meal she had cooked.

He had declined her offer of lunch and usually had many meetings on Sundays after church, but she reckoned if Pastor Tom could take time to go home with his family for lunch, then John could take an hour out of his busy schedule to eat with his wife! When she arrived, Mabel was there again, this time without her children. She brought some African food, wanting to feed John and spend time with him!

"I see you're here again," Victoria said as she lifted Mabel's picnic basket, put it on the floor beside the desk, and set hers in its place. She beamed when she was done. "Where're your daughters?"

Mabel returned the smile, but Victoria could tell she was uncomfortable as she shifted uneasily in her chair and glanced at John, who paced the room, speaking on the phone to a member he was counselling.

"I left them at home. They need to prepare for school tomorrow."

"Of course. It's a school night. You probably will want to rush home to them."

Mabel got the message and hurriedly left. Victoria wanted to call her attention to the fact that she was leaving her picnic basket behind, but she decided against it. She didn't want John to think she was being petty. The woman brought him food as other women did, but Victoria did not intend to let her sit there and eat with her husband.

In the early days of her marriage, she would have become upset and demanded an explanation as to why Mabel thought it was her place to bring John food. John would have said that she was a woman who understood how to honour a man of God, unlike the woman he married. They would have argued back and forth, and John would have told her she had a long way to go in her walk with the Lord. He would have accused her of being like worldly women with no regard and honour for their husbands.

So, after Mabel's departure, she said nothing. She laid out the contents of her picnic basket, and she and John sat down to eat. It was a nice meal; they focused on themselves without talking about the children, the church, or its members. But as they talked, she found it hard to stop thinking about what Mabel was like. Mabel wanted her husband. She gave him a come-hither look that made Victoria confident she was trouble. She appeared unassuming, almost foolish, but Victoria thought her humility was a cover. Mabel Babs-Jonah was nobody's fool but a calculating woman who, if left unchecked, had the potential to overstep her boundaries with another woman's husband.

Victoria longed to tell John that Mabel sought more than just a pastor and spiritual mentor; but worried John would accuse her of jealousy and delusion. The matter was eating her up. She returned home hoping to regain her calm and composure, but she was faced with the possibility that she was failing in her duty as a mother. Her whole world seemed to crumble. She would have to pay closer attention to Rebekah and Paul. John Jr. not so much, as he needed little supervision or encouragement for his walk with the Lord. In that regard, he was his father's son. Paul and Rebekah were the ones more likely to yield to peer pressure.

Victoria wished John would support her more with raising the children. She lacked complete understanding and didn't have all the answers. But what time did he have? Mabel and her children alone were a full-time job, never mind other women in the church who didn't have husbands to help them raise their kids. He was the hero of every woman except the woman he married.

She let out a sigh. That wasn't accurate. He had been her hero once. Victoria recalled her first impression of John. He was so tall and handsome that she fell in love with him on sight. She did everything John wanted. John wanted her to be born again, so she became born again. As she hung around him and experienced the confidence with which he operated in the miraculous, she fell more and more in love with him. When John proposed, she thought she had hit the jackpot. She wanted one child; he wanted three, so she wanted three. But after being unable to conceive after two years, she feared she wouldn't even be able to have one, never mind three. John remained unperturbed.

"We're going to have three children. A girl, and then two boys. That's my covenant with God."

Victoria looked at him in bewilderment. She thought he was crazy and unlike anyone she'd met. Then she booked a medical examination and, after a couple of weeks, received an infertility diagnosis. She wept bitterly that she would not be able to give the man she loved the children he desired. Then John came home, and just before they retired for the night, she passed him the report.

"What's this?" he asked, looking up from the Christian fiction novel he was reading just before bed.

"It's the report from my physical exam and lab tests," she said, still holding the report towards him.

He put down his novel and reached for the report. It listed numerous infertility issues, from endometriosis to premature ovarian failure. Victoria held her breath as he looked at the report, wondering what he would do next. What he did, she least expected.

John tore the report to shreds and tossed it into the bin by his bedside. Victoria gasped. "Why did you do that?"

He turned to look at her as if she'd grown two heads. "Do you want those things listed in that report?"

"It's not about whether I want them!" she argued. "Of course, I don't want them. But I have them!"

"Not anymore," John said, picking up his novel and continuing to read. Victoria stared at him, not sure what to say. After a moment, he looked at her. "I told you we're having three children, and that is the end of that. You don't need to have faith. I have faith. Our children will come in God's time."

John was right. Rebekah was born within a year of that night, and John Jr. followed the next year. The speed with which she conceived John Jr. made her opt for the pill, and years later, when she thought she was ready and came off the pill, she became pregnant with Paul almost immediately. Her children were a testament to the power John operated in as a man of God. He was her hero. This made him attractive to her, and she would be a fool to think it didn't attract other women. It was for this reason that the women worshipped him. And when they flocked around him, he couldn't help but give them attention. She should be used to it by now, but she wasn't.

Her mobile phone rang, and she stood up, looking around for it. It was still in her handbag, so she retrieved it and returned to sit on the vanity stool. Her sister Anna was calling, and Victoria's face lit up. Anna was just the person she needed to get her mind off things.

"Anna! How are you? How are Mum and Sarah?"

"Everyone is excellent!" Anna's high-pitched voice was strong and full of life. Her strength, confidence, and positivity brought a smile to Victoria's face.

Victoria's sister, Anna, was six years her senior and had recently lost her husband, Jack, after over two decades of marriage. With Sarah, Anna's only child, grown and independent, their widowed mother had moved from Australia to Texas to help Anna run the ranch and resort she had co-owned with Jack.

Victoria was impressed by Anna's ability to recover from the loss of her love and resume her life. Victoria's marriage to John brought her family to Christ, and this strengthened Anna's positive attitude. Though widowed for just nine months, she persistently pursued her dreams. Her zest for life prevented anyone from feeling sorry for her.

"How are things going with you, John, and the kids?" Anna asked. "And how's that megachurch of yours?"

Over a month had passed since Victoria last spoke with Anna or their mother; their days were so busy that previous calls had been rushed and unsatisfying. Before then, Anna was the focus because of her husband's passing. Many months had passed since she meaningfully conversed with either woman, and she missed their company, particularly Anna's.

"We are doing very well, and the megachurch is prospering." A faint smile touched Victoria's lips. "It's kind of you to call."

"Kind? Vicky, is everything okay?" Anna asked, picking up on Victoria's lack of excitement right away. "You don't seem thrilled to hear from me, if I'm being honest. What's going on? Talk to me."

Lost in thought, Victoria chewed on her bottom lip. She wasn't sure whether to update Anna on current events. What would be the point? What issue would it resolve? During the initial years of her marriage, she shared her concerns with her sister, who advised her to pray for and be patient with John. Anna might give the same advice now, which Victoria would not find helpful, and it may not solve the problem; however, Victoria believed talking about it would be beneficial.

"Well, it's not anything that you aren't aware of. It's John and his schedules that leave no time for his immediate family. You probably think I should be used to it by now, and perhaps I should, but I'm not. And I don't see it getting any better. There's also the issue of a new woman in the church who may be overstepping where John's concerned."

Victoria relayed all her knowledge of Mabel Babs-Jonah and the day's events to Anna. On the other end of the phone, silence reigned as Anna pondered her reply.

"Have you spoken to John recently about spending more time with you and the kids, and have you called his attention to how this woman's behaviour is inappropriate?"

Anna knew more than anyone else that Victoria had spoken to John about his failure to spend enough time with her and the children. His response was always to portray her as a selfish, self-centred woman who didn't want her husband to help others.

"I haven't spoken to him recently because I already anticipate his response, and I don't have the energy for a fight. If it weren't for this woman and her apparent interest in John, I would carry on without complaining."

Again, Anna remained silent at the other end of the phone as she took in Victoria's words. After a while, she spoke again.

"Why don't you and the kids come to the ranch in Texas for a week this summer?" she suggested. "Mum and I would love to have you visit. And I'm sure Sarah will make the time to be around for your visit. We'll have so much fun together. The change of environment will do you some good, and perhaps John may decide to come with you, and you could seize the opportunity to turn it into a nice second honeymoon away from church and the commitments to the brethren."

A dry laugh escaped Victoria's lips. "Thank you for the offer, Anna. I accept it because a change of environment is probably what I need right now. Being able to see you, Mum, and Sarah will be great, and the children would love a holiday at the ranch. As for John coming with us or me turning it into a second honeymoon, I can assure you there is more hope of a camel going through the eye of a needle."

CHAPTER SEVEN

Two months later…

"You're late," Barry snapped as his friend and business partner, Lanre Fischer, leisurely slid a chair back from the beautifully set table in their favourite exquisite Yoruba restaurant.

The aroma of spices wafted through the air, and with a contented sigh, Lanre settled into his seat, ready for an evening filled with delicious flavours and business conversations.

"My sincere apologies. I got held up in a meeting." He eyed Barry. "You look like your day was as bad as mine."

Barry groaned and sipped his drink. "Don't go there. I don't want to talk about it."

"I hear you." Lanre glanced around the softly lit diner. "Where's Dele, by the way?"

Dele Ajala, the third member of their trio, who'd been a bachelor playboy for years, was on his honeymoon after recently getting married. His honeymoon was extended, so he could not be with them tonight.

Barry frowned. "Didn't he tell you?"

Lanre looked puzzled. "Tell me what?"

"He's extended his honeymoon by one more week."

Lanre, a chronic bachelor, was greatly displeased. He contorted his face. "Ugh. He already had two weeks."

Barry shrugged. "So now it'll be three. We can't say he hasn't earned the time off." He signalled to the waiter.

Lanre shook his head. "He's acting like a love-sick fool. One week is sufficient for a honeymoon; two is an overkill. Three is just downright crazy." He picked up the menu.

"Yeah," Barry muttered under his breath. "I can't wait until he's been with her a few years, and she's packed on the pounds or refused to develop her mind."

Lanre opened his mouth to speak but closed it again as the waiter arrived. They ordered their dinner, and as the waiter walked away, Lanre put down the menu and pulled out his phone.

"Bro, you're not going to believe what I stumbled upon on social media. Facebook, to be precise."

Barry eyed him as he flicked through his phone. "What did you stumble on?"

"A picture of Mabel."

Barry let out his breath with a hissing sound. He didn't want to discuss Mabel. Lanre knew this. He had blocked her everywhere. His assistant sent her a huge sum of money monthly so the girls lacked nothing. He didn't want to hear about her and avoided her family and friends.

He also stayed away from Manchester now residing in the Bromley area of Greater London.

"Lanre, you know how I feel about discussing Mabel."

"Wait until you see this." Lanre handed him the phone, and Barry saw a photo of Mabel with the girls. The photo was taken in a church, and she wrote about being blessed by the sermon. There was a man beside her with his arm around her shoulder; Barry learned from the post that he was Pastor John.

Barry gazed at the photo, disbelief washing over him as he tried to comprehend what he was seeing. Mabel had lost all the weight she had gained during their seventeen-year marriage. Her dress, cinched at the waist, revealed a flat tummy, small waist, and hourglass figure. She looked like a different person. It was like looking at another woman. He licked his lips to moisten them as he passed the phone back to Lanre.

"She looks great, doesn't she?" Lanre asked, and without waiting for an answer, he added, "I saw the picture and thought, wow, she won't have a problem remarrying. She looks so young, it's hard to tell Tracy and Stacy are her daughters."

Barry picked up his glass of water and took a sip. "She'll soon pack on the pounds again."

He was grateful when the waiter arrived with their drinks and then their food. The conversation quickly changed after that to business, the reason for the meeting in the first place. But as they discussed, he only half-heartedly listened as he pondered how to access Mabel's social media posts. He must know exactly what she was getting up to. She may no longer be his wife, but he wasn't paying her a huge sum of money each month to look pretty for another man.

Elizabeth expertly manoeuvred her sleek BMW into position in front of the charming two-storey red brick house that belonged to the Campbells. The warm hues of the brick contrasted beautifully with the lush greenery surrounding the home, giving it an inviting aura. She turned to look at the quiet but enraged mixed-race teen in the front passenger seat of her car. His arms folded across his chest and in a defiant pose, Oliver Campbell stayed quiet through the ride from the police station. The area around his left eye where he'd been hit during a pub fight was already turning into a nasty bruise.

He would be a handsome boy if he lost the foul attitude, Elizabeth thought as she studied him, wondering what angered him. He got into a fight and inconvenienced herself and Anita by making them drive to the station instead of going home to their kids or getting on with other things on their itinerary.

John called her at work to inform her that the police had arrested nineteen-year-old Oliver, Audrey's youngest son, for getting in a fight at a pub. Oliver needed a lawyer, and as she wasn't a criminal defence solicitor, she took Anita with her, and together, they attended the police station. Anita stayed with Oliver as the police questioned him, while Elizabeth remained in the waiting room.

He'd been released without charge. As Anita explained, the police needed time to review the evidence.

He may be asked to return to the station but for now, he was free.

"You're home now, Oliver. Go in and stay out of trouble," she said.

"Thank you," he mumbled but made no move to get out.

"Is there something wrong, Oliver?" Elizabeth asked.

For the next minute, Oliver expressed his frustration about how the police treated him during his arrest.

"Did you tell Anita all this?" Elizabeth cut in when he wouldn't shut up.

"Yes, I did, Miss Elizabeth. I told her everything. She told the police she took issue with their use of excessive force during my apprehension. They said they used reasonable force. Reasonable force, my foot!"

"Were you resisting arrest?"

"No!" Oliver looked outraged that she would ask such a question.

"You leave it with Anita. If anything is amiss in the arrest process, she will deal with it accordingly."

"I should certainly hope so, Miss Elizabeth. Those men used excessive force when arresting me, and it wasn't necessary because I didn't try to resist arrest. But I know why they did it."

"Yeah?" Elizabeth asked with a raised brow.

"Yeah. It's because I'm black, Miss Elizabeth." He turned and glared at Elizabeth. "It's because I'm black, Miss Elizabeth, isn't it?"

With a sigh and a head shake, Elizabeth contemplated a smack to Oliver Campbell's face. If only it would impart some wisdom. "No, Oliver. It's not because you're black. It's because you're a fool."

The answer he received was unexpected. Oliver stared at her, dumbfounded. Elizabeth jerked her head in the direction of the house. "Go on. Your parents are waiting for you."

With a scowl and a matching attitude, Oliver exited the car and closed the door behind him without a backward glance or a thank you. Elizabeth rolled her eyes as she steered her car off the curb and back onto the road.

She pushed Oliver from her mind as she drove to Barry's home, her body humming with excitement at the thought of what lay ahead. She had anticipated this meeting since their last. It wouldn't be the first time she'd taken paperwork to him to sign at home, and they'd had sex. She and Barry had a great sexual life and could hardly keep their hands off each other, turning every meeting into a sexual encounter. He was also as excited to see her because the moment she stepped through his front door, he grabbed her and pulled her to him.

"Finally, we're alone," he said as his mouth covered hers and his powerful arms encircled her slender waist like a vice, holding her tightly against his body.

Elizabeth's handbag and envelope with the documents slipped from her grasp and landed on the floor, and she wrapped her arms around his neck, angling her head and deepening the kiss even as he picked her up and carried her to the bedroom, where he proceeded to take off her clothes like a starving man.

An hour later, she was showered and dressed, and Barry signed the papers and handed them back to her.

"Are we still good for the New York trip next week?" he asked as he walked her to the front door.

"I wouldn't miss it for the world." Elizabeth winked at him and blew him a kiss before she stepped out of the house and hurried to her car.

Barry watched as Elizabeth climbed into her car and drove away. He furrowed his brows as he stepped back inside the hallway and shut the door behind him. With his hands buried deep in the pockets of his silk dressing gown, he walked slowly into the living room and reflected on their time together. Elizabeth was a beautiful and intelligent woman; the sex was great, and while he enjoyed it immensely, it was just that—sex.

He wasn't ready to take their relationship further. Truth be told, he was already getting bored and seeking a replacement. His mind returned to Mabel and her new appearance, and he scratched his bristly chin. He decided to find out what she was up to. He picked up his phone and called his assistant.

"Steve, I want you to send me screenshots of everything Mabel has posted online in the last year—everything from all social media accounts. I don't think I need to tell you to be discreet. Start sending them yesterday. I am waiting. Impatiently."

"You have got to be kidding me!"

Elizabeth punched her steering wheel in frustration. Oh, how she hated these electric cars. They were useless—the lot of them. What did she do now? Her car had suddenly died. And it had chosen the wrong place to do so—the Queen Elizabeth II Bridge. It had chosen the wrong time—11 p.m. What was worse was that her breakdown company wasn't going to do anything about it.

"Call the police," they told her. "We can't come out there. It's a dangerous location!"

"But I pay you to show up in such situations," she argued.

"Yes, and normally we would. But you are in a dangerous location. My suggestion is that you call the police."

"I don't need the police! I need you to come and get me out of here!"

The argument lasted a few more minutes, and after yelling and cursing, she ended the call. She could not believe it. They were not coming.

Call the police?

She stared at her phone in utter disbelief. These people were unbelievable. She didn't need the police. She needed someone to come and fix her car or get it towed and provide her with some transportation to get home. That's what she paid the useless breakdown company for.

She thought of Barry. He was always so resourceful and would tell her what to do. With a spark of excitement in her eyes and a playful smile dancing across her lips, she dialled his mobile number.

"My apologies, sweetheart, but I have a business call with some Japanese partners to join shortly," Barry said after she explained that her car had broken down and she needed his help. Without waiting for her response, he hung up.

With a mix of shock and incredulity, she fixed her gaze on the phone yet again, unable to comprehend what just happened. What was wrong with everybody today? How could Barry end the call, aware that she was stranded in a broken-down car? What meeting was he referring to? He mentioned no such meeting while she was with him less than an hour ago.

She shrugged, speculating that something had come up. Then, she dialled John's number, hoping that John would be able to tell her what to do. But the phone rang and proceeded directly to voicemail. She sighed and cut the call without leaving a message.

What now? she wondered. *How did she get out of this unpleasant situation?*

This wasn't a situation she had been faced with before and left to deal with on her own. Chris always took care of such matters. What was her understanding of automobiles besides operating them? Chris looked after her car and guided her on how to navigate difficult situations. Perhaps she could call him now? She screwed up her face.

In the two months since Chris left home, their interactions were infrequent. He came by whenever the boys needed him, and he ensured they had everything they needed. He was courteous to her the few times they spoke, but that didn't mean he would jump to her rescue. She had not exactly given him reason to continue to be her knight in shining armour.

But Chris loved her. She was confident that he did. It was in his eyes every time he glanced in her direction, and he had always looked after her. Would that suddenly change because he'd moved out of the house? Well, there was no need to think and overthink things. If Chris would help her, he would, and if he wouldn't, then she would know not to bother him in the future.

She took a deep breath and tried to steady her shaky hands as she dialled his number. He answered on the first ring as if he'd been sitting with the phone in his hand, waiting for her call. Her lips formed a gentle smile. Chris, her very own knight in shining armour, never failed to come to her rescue.

"Hey, Elizabeth. What's going on?" Chris knew she wouldn't call him at this odd hour of the night if the matter weren't serious. He probably thought it concerned the boys. Well, in a way, it did. She needed to get home to them. The childminder was currently watching them. Twenty-one-year-old Ava lived across the street from them, and as she was in university and looking for extra money, Elizabeth often asked her to watch the boys in the evenings.

"My car is dead, Chris. I'm at a loss as to what I should do." She told him how her breakdown company refused to come out to her because they claimed the area was dangerous.

Chris sighed. "Okay. I'm on my way."

She couldn't believe it. He neither argued nor complained. But then that was Chris. The ideal father and husband. Well, he would be the ideal husband and father if he got his business together again. She didn't want a man who was not ambitious or too afraid to get up and try again after a setback. Chris' lack of ambition was her issue with him.

And it was major because as much as she wanted a man to come every time she called for him, she also wanted him to be successful, someone she could be proud of. Someone like Barry, even though Barry didn't care that she was unable to get home in the middle of the night. She frowned as she recalled how curt he sounded on the phone. Chris had never spoken to her like that. She couldn't even imagine him speaking to her like that. Chris worshipped the ground that she walked on.

Elizabeth was so lost in her thoughts that she didn't realise how much time had flown by until she saw Chris's Jaguar SUV pulled up in front of her BMW. Ever the gentleman, he got out of his car and helped her out of hers. Elizabeth experienced an urge to step into his arms, but she held herself back. She wasn't with Chris anymore. She was with Barry now.

Yes? *And where is he*? The voice in her head taunted her, and she shut it down as she said a quick hello to Chris and locked her car before climbing into his for the ride home.

"Thank you, Chris. I'm grateful for your help. In hindsight, I could have simply called a taxi or Uber."

Chris shrugged as he pulled his vehicle onto the road, glancing at her vehicle one more time through the rearview mirror. He knew why Elizabeth called him. For the period they'd been together, she relied heavily on him to keep her life running smoothly. Beneath the high-powered career woman profile lay a vulnerable woman who needed a strong man to lean on. Elizabeth was easily stressed when things didn't go according to plan.

She was unfamiliar with handling unexpected events such as car breakdowns. Chris believed the event had been entirely avoidable. This situation would only have arisen because, in her characteristic nature, Elizabeth ignored the warning signs. She didn't need to take care of such matters when he lived at home because he ensured her car was up and running. All she did was drive.

"You weren't thinking straight because you were stressed. I'm glad you called me."

He meant it. He may have left their home, but he still considered her his woman, his to look after, protect, and provide for.

Elizabeth turned to look at him. He took his eyes off the road for a fraction of a second, and their eyes met and held. She looked away quickly. At that moment, her phone rang, and she pulled it out of her handbag, thankful for the distraction. It was John.

"Hi, Elizabeth. I'm sorry I missed your call. Is everything okay? Audrey called me to say you dropped Oliver off at home. I can't thank you enough."

"You're welcome, John. But I didn't call because of Oliver. My car died, and I thought you could advise me on what to do."

"You've got breakdown cover; call the company," he said.

"I did that, and they wouldn't come. Not at this time of the night. That's why I called you."

"You could have called a taxi to take you home."

Elizabeth sighed and rolled her eyes. "I realise that now. I was too panicked to think of that."

"Yes. Because Chris has spoilt you."

Elizabeth was glad the call was not on speaker. She glanced at Chris and pondered what John said.

"You'll be happy to know I'm safe. Chris came to get me and is taking me home."

Silence fell on the line for a while, and Elizabeth frowned, wondering if the connection had been lost or if he hadn't heard her.

"The man is too good for you, Elizabeth," John said. "I'm glad you're safe. Good night."

She stared at the phone for a moment before putting it in her bag.

"John giving you grief?" Chris asked, causing Elizabeth to turn and look at him.

She smiled and shrugged. "You know John."

"I do," he chuckled. "Who's minding the kids?"

Elizabeth was glad of the change of topic. "Ava is with them. The poor thing. She's probably already dozed off on the sofa."

"Good thing she only has to cross the road to get home."

"Yeah," Elizabeth agreed, stifling a yawn. "It makes me feel a lot better knowing that. I didn't plan to be home so late today. It was just one of those days."

"We all have them. The days when nothing goes to plan."

"Today was that kind of day. I worked a little late, and then John called asking me to go to the station as Oliver Campbell needed a lawyer." She didn't mention her appointment with a client after dropping Oliver at home. She couldn't mention that, not when the client was her lover, and she'd just experienced passionate intimacy with him.

"Oh, I see. I was wondering why you mentioned Oliver earlier." He shook his head. "So Oliver is still up to his shenanigans?"

"Yes. Oliver is still up to his shenanigans. This time, it was a fight in a pub. I took Anita with me when John called, as she's a criminal defence lawyer."

"How did it go?"

Elizabeth shrugged. "He was released without charge. I drove him home. Hopefully, he stays out of trouble."

"And you were on your way back when your car died."

"Yep!" There was no way she was going to mention Barry. Absolutely not.

"What a day!" Chris's dramatic expression and grin made Elizabeth laugh.

He turned to her as they pulled up in front of the house. "Give me your car keys, and I'll tow the car in the morning. It's either run out of battery or has a hardware or software issue. Either way, I'll sort it out and hopefully have it ready for you before the end of the day."

Elizabeth handed him the key. "Thank you, Chris."

"You're welcome."

He walked her to the front door, and as she entered, Ava came to the foyer, smiling as she saw them both. She looked nerdy but charming in her oversized eyeglasses, jeans, a long-sleeved T-shirt with her university's name inscribed on the front of it, and Converse trainers. Her bright red hair was in a ponytail, tousled from sleep.

"Hello, Elizabeth. Hello Chris."

"I am so sorry for keeping you so late, Ava."

"That's okay. The boys have gone to bed." She threw her arms above her head and stretched.

"Thank you, Ava. You are my superstar," Elizabeth said, placing her bag and files on the console to avoid knocking down the large antique vase. She removed her trench coat to reveal a short-sleeved black dress that flattered her figure and a string of South Sea pearls with a diamond clasp. "I hope they were good?"

Ava chuckled. "They're always good, Elizabeth."

"Come on, Ava," Chris said. "I'll walk you to your door."

"I'm just across the road. You don't have to," Ava said, reaching inside the cloakroom for her denim jacket and putting it on.

"Oh, I insist." Chris frowned and shoved his hands inside the pockets of his bomber jacket.

Ava laughed, grabbed her backpack, and put it on. "Okay. Fine. Knight in shining armour." She turned towards Elizabeth. "Good night, Elizabeth."

"Good night, Ava. Thank you again."

Elizabeth stood by the open doorway and watched Chris and Ava walk hand in hand across the street towards Ava's front door. She frowned as Chris's hand transferred to the small of Ava's back, as he gently pushed her inside the house. She shut the front door, her heart beating a little wildly in her chest. Was there something happening between Chris and Ava? In her pursuit of Barry, had she missed the telltale signals of an affair happening under her nose? Or was it all innocent?

CHAPTER EIGHT

Four weeks later…

"Yes, Dad. I love you too, Dad. Bye, Dad."

Mabel walked into Tracy's bedroom just as Tracy ended the call and froze to the spot, her mouth hanging open. What was that she just heard? Had Tracy addressed the caller as Dad? She blinked as she tried to comprehend what was going on. Could that have been Barry? Was Barry in contact with Tracy? If he was, why didn't Tracy say anything? And for how long had this been going on?

"Who was that?" With a frown and narrowed eyes, she pointed at the device in Tracy's hand.

Tracy averted her gaze; guilt etched across her features. She slipped the mobile phone into the back pocket of her jeans as though she feared Mabel would reach out and take it from her hands.

"It was Dad." She said after what appeared to be an eternity.

Mabel folded her arms across her chest. "Dad?" she asked in utter disbelief. She hoped she had misheard, hoped there was a mistake. "Dad?"

Tracy threw her hands up in the air. "Mum, it's not what you think."

Mabel raised an eyebrow. "Pray tell, what do I think?"

Tracy was at a loss for words. She gnawed her bottom lip and tugged on a braid, twisting it around her index finger. "Sorry, Mum."

"Sorry?" Mabel asked. "What are you sorry for? Are you sorry for communicating with your father without my knowledge, or are you sorry I found out you've been communicating with your father behind my back?" When Tracy didn't answer, she continued. "How long have you been in contact with your father? And why the secrecy? Have I said you can't communicate with your father?"

"He called me on my mobile for the first time yesterday. He said he missed us and wanted to enquire about our welfare. I didn't want to keep it a secret, but he said he would call you to arrange to spend time with me and my sisters once we vacate for the summer holiday in three weeks." Tracy explained, wringing her fingers.

Mabel nodded slowly; she looked at Tracy but didn't see her. Barry had surfaced to find out how his children were. Once again, she would have to deal with him. She had known this day would come; she just hadn't known when. After packing up and leaving suddenly, she hadn't known if he intended to continue to be a father to his kids or just provide for them from a distance until they were adults and could interact with him without her involvement.

She was the one Barry didn't want. The girls only suffered his rejection because they were young and could not communicate with their father without her. And Barry wanted nothing to do with her. He called Tracy yesterday and told Tracy he would call her. But he didn't call her even though he called Tracy again today.

She snapped out of her reverie as she realised Tracy was speaking.

"I also told him that Daisy's been feeling unwell lately and is booked to see the GP again next week. Perhaps I shouldn't have. I'm sorry, Mum." Tears welled in her eyes as she spoke in a near whisper.

Mabel pulled her into an embrace.

"I know you didn't mean any harm." She wiped Tracy's tears with her thumbs. "Next time he calls to inquire about the happenings in this house, ask him to call me. Tell him I said so. Okay?"

"Okay, Mum." Tracy nodded with a smile.

"I need you downstairs to help serve dinner. Daisy won't join us. I just fed her in bed and gave her some paracetamol to ease the joint pains. She's out for the count."

"Is she feeling better, then?"

"Yes, she is. She should be able to go to school tomorrow." Mabel turned and walked away, pausing at the door. "And pick all of this stuff up off the floor, Tracy. The cleaner was here only this morning."

"Sorry." Tracy grinned apologetically as she scurried around the room, picking her school bag and its contents from the pink carpeted floor. "I never know how my things find their way to the floor."

Mabel sighed exasperatedly and walked away; Tracy's giggle trailed her as she descended the stairs.

After dinner, with the girls in bed, Mabel sat in the small box room she converted into an office and logged into her school portal to do some preparation tasks ahead of her classes the following day. She struggled to concentrate, and her mind returned to her conversation with Tracy.

She was still in shock that Barry had been in touch with them. His behaviour was still a shock to her, and although she tried to pretend it didn't bother her anymore, the truth was it did. Of course, it did. She was married to Barry for seventeen years. He claimed to love her. Granted, the marriage hadn't been a bed of roses; which marriage was? But they'd had very happy times, and she believed they would be together forever. Barry complained about her weight and lack of drive to develop herself, but she hadn't seen it as a serious problem, and she didn't believe it was something he would leave her and the girls over.

Her father complained about many things her mother did, but he never quit his family over those things. She always thought that men quit their families when their wives were unfaithful or when they fell in love with another woman. She had never been unfaithful to Barry, and as for him leaving for another woman, while she suspected he may have had affairs as he never took her on any business trips, she was confident that he loved her. So, yes, one year later, she was still greatly distressed by his desertion.

Now that he was back and talking with Tracy, she knew it was only a matter of time before he called her, especially since she had told Tracy not to share any information with him but to ask him to call her. Was she ready to talk to him? A year ago, she would have given anything to communicate with him, but now she wasn't so sure. Her life was changing very quickly.

Day by day, she grew more beautiful and self-assured. When she did the school run, men turned to look at her, and even other mothers on the school run turned to look at her. Pastor John spoke to her about not being a slob, and she dressed nicely every morning before driving the girls to school, styling her hair, putting on some makeup, and wearing her perfume.

Her pride extended beyond her physical attractiveness. She was doing very well on her business degree course and excelling in her business. People couldn't get enough of the beautiful clothes *Ara* made, and large orders came through her website daily placed by individuals and retailers.

Since Barry left more than a year ago, she'd grown considerably and accomplished much. It was necessary to consider how his involvement in her life would disrupt things. Her current life was not one she wanted to be disrupted. If Barry's return led to issues like visitation demands or custody battles, she'd rather he stayed away.

Her phone rang, and she shifted her gaze from the laptop screen to the device where it lay on her desk. The number was unknown. Her heart skipped a beat. Barry. It must be Barry. Who else would it be? She had very few friends, having distanced herself from her friends in Manchester. And if her friends in Manchester called, their numbers wouldn't come up as unknown.

Mabel took a deep breath as she picked up the phone with a shaky hand and answered the call.

"Mabel, it's Barry." Barry's deep voice travelled to her from the other end of the line.

"Good evening, Barry." Mabel shut her eyes and tried to calm herself.

God, give me strength, she prayed. She could not escape Barry. For the girls, she needed to interact with him, and required strength to keep him out of her heart for good.

He's no longer your husband, Mabel. Remember that, she chided.

Barry chuckled. "You sound awfully polite."

Mabel prayed again for strength because, at that moment, a part of her wanted to reach into the phone and wallop him on the head with a saucepan. She pushed back her pale pink velvet swivel chair and crossed her legs.

"What can I do for you, Barry?"

Barry Babs-Jonah pulled the phone away from his ear and stared at it. Yes, he had dialled the right number. The word "Wifey" boldly displayed on his screen confirmed that. He never changed how he stored Mabel's number on his phone and didn't want to consider why that was. Not when Mabel sounded very distant. Had she not missed him? Her tone revealed no excitement. He hadn't anticipated her excitement level to match Tracy's, or to sound like she was catching up with a long-lost friend.

He was not a friend. The moment he walked out on their marriage and ended it, he ceased to be a friend. But Mabel adored him until that point, and he learned that she struggled to cope with his leaving and was hospitalised. So why was she now acting like he was a total stranger? Had she become so indifferent to him in a year? Who was this woman acting cool, classy and unbothered? Mabel, with her vulgar and unrefined manners, was nowhere to be seen. Why was she not screaming and swearing at him in Yoruba?

"I wanted to find out how you're doing," he said in answer to her question. Why else would he call?

"That's very kind of you, Barry. I'm sure Tracy has informed you that we are well."

Barry grimaced. How did she know about that? He asked Tracy not to say anything.

While he pondered the matter, Mabel spoke again. "I walked in on her talking to you earlier this evening."

"I needed to know how you were. How you all were." He walked to the drinks cabinet and poured himself a shot of brandy. This call wasn't going as he'd anticipated, he decided as he raised the glass to his lips.

"You could have called me Barry. You and I may have our differences, but you are the girls' father, and I'm happy to accommodate you should you wish to pursue a relationship with them."

Barry again lowered the phone and stared at the screen to ensure he had dialled the correct number. He had. The word "Wifey" was still displayed on the screen. But who was this stranger talking to him? This was not Mabel. Mabel would be crying by now, accusing him of ruining her life, cursing him out in Yoruba, or forbidding him from getting in touch with the girls. She would have raised her voice like a crude market woman. But she hadn't. She sounded cool, calm, and collected. A part of him wished she would show some emotion, and then he would be confident she still cared.

But she must still care. It had only been a year and a few months. She couldn't have shut him out of her heart in a year, not after what they had shared in seventeen years.

What had they shared in seventeen years? he asked himself.

He was away a lot of the time, taking women with him as he travelled and paying little attention to his wife. Her indifference hadn't been built in the last year; it took seventeen years of his indifference to bring her to this place of nonchalance. He swallowed his drink and savoured the burning sensation that struck the back of his throat.

"Thank you. That is good to know. I let Tracy know that I'd love to spend time with her, Stacy, and Daisy during the summer break."

"She relayed your message. It's fine. I think it's just what the girls need. And it would free me up for some *me* time."

Barry frowned. Just what did she plan to do with her *me* time? She'd lost weight and looked great after he left—something she'd never done for him—making him believe she had a new in her life. He wanted to ask, but he changed his mind.

Don't sound desperate and pathetic, Barry, he warned. *Be cool*.

"I understand that you moved from Manchester."

Mabel held out her hand, admiring her newly manicured nails with their French tips. "So did you," she reminded him.

He laughed drily. "Yes. You're right." He raised his glass once more and drank.

"Well, if that's all for now, Barry, I will say good night."

"I thought that perhaps we could have dinner soon."

"Whatever you want, Barry," Mabel said nonchalantly. "If you're ever in London and want to catch up for a meal, take the girls to a movie, or for the weekend, I'm happy to oblige you. Enjoy the rest of your evening.

After Mabel ended the call, Barry stared at his phone, sick to the stomach. Mabel wasn't putting up an act. She didn't care. His phone rang. It was Elizabeth, and he smiled. Just the person to boost his ego. He needed to see her now. She would improve his spirits.

"Hey, babe." Her smooth voice flowed through the line.

"Where are you? I need to see you tonight." He wasted no time getting to the point.

She laughed delightfully, her mirth echoing through the phone line. "I'm still in the office. But I leave in an hour. I will come straight to yours."

"Good. Plan to stay the night."

"I will."

He ended the call and drained the contents of his glass. Elizabeth's readiness for sex always excited him. Mabel could go to hell. He had no time for whatever stupid game she was trying to play.

Mabel put her phone down and wiped tears from her eyes. How dare he call and act as though they were old friends reconnecting? How dare he talk to her as if he had not deeply hurt her? Did he really think he could treat her like she was insignificant, entering and exiting her life at will? As if she had no feelings or as if they didn't matter? Barry Babs-Jonah was a monster, but he would soon understand that the old Mabel was gone.

She picked up her phone and called Pastor John. His voice, wise words, and laughter would soothe the pain in her heart. Such an exceptional man, he was; she envied his wife.

CHAPTER NINE

John steered his Range Rover off the bustling road and onto the winding drive that led to his home. As he rolled to a stop in front of the house, a sense of calm washed over him, the day's stresses fading with each turn of the wheels. The familiar sight of his sanctuary welcomed him, inviting him to leave the world behind for a while. He switched off the engine and reached for his phone, calling Pastor Tom, who had been with him all day and shown strong support for him during his visit to members of The Vine Church in crisis.

"Hey Tom, I'm just checking to see if you got home okay," he said as soon as the familiar voice came on the line.

"Yes, I did. Thank you for checking."

"My pleasure. And thank you for coming out with me today. Your presence was a great source of comfort."

"Anytime, John."

"Give my love to Blossom."

As he ended the call, he rested his head against the headrest, shut his eyes, and exhaled deeply as he contemplated the day's events. Being a pastor had its positive and negative sides. Today, it seemed he had seen all the negative sides. His visitation had begun in the hospital to comfort a woman in her forties who'd had a stillbirth. She and her husband were committed members of the church.

They'd been married for a decade and trusted God for a child. After years of miscarriages and countless prayers, she'd become pregnant and carried the pregnancy to full term, only to have a stillbirth due to umbilical cord problems. She had been inconsolable. Not even his presence or assurance that God would turn her mourning into dancing had comforted her. It had been heartbreaking to watch, a reality of the battles the believer was called to fight. He had left the hospital despondent.

With Pastor Tom at his side, he had made the second visit to offer pastoral support to a couple grieving the loss of their only son. The young man had committed suicide following pressure from his mother to get a job and the constant comparison to his mates. It had been a challenging visit, like the first one. The woman was broken, her spirit broken. He could tell she would never recover from knowing she had driven her son to suicide.

Then there was the husband. He had looked calm the entire time and responded positively as John encouraged them both from God's word. But he knew the man had decided to leave his wife. John could tell, watching him, that he blamed her for the death of his only son. He prayed with them, yet his spirit remained troubled.

The young man would be buried in a few days. As their pastor, he would officiate the ceremony. It would give him time again to pray and encourage them from God's word. He would invite the entire church to pray for them at the midweek Bible study tomorrow. They needed prayers and God's intervention and comfort to prevent the marriage from failing and the demise of the already broken woman. She had aged more than a decade. It broke his heart to watch her. Like most mothers, all she wanted was the best for her son. How was she to know her nagging would drive him to take his own life?

The third family was a family of two. A single mother, Abigail, was on the verge of losing her only child, Lily. He knew the family well, as he had supported Abigail emotionally and spiritually when she joined The Vine Church about five years ago. Lily was an only child born out of wedlock to a man who, although he had been living with Abigail at the time, had returned to his wife and kids just before the birth of Lily, leaving Abigail to go through the last stages of her pregnancy and the birth alone. She was a broken woman when he met her, lacking in confidence and a complete pushover. Even Lily intimidated her and was spoilt, a child out of control, being allowed to do anything she wanted, which landed them in this mess.

Unknown to Abigail, fourteen-year-old Lily had uploaded a nude video of herself online. The authorities had become aware, and yesterday, the police and social services paid an unannounced visit to the home, interrogating mother and child. Their findings revealed that Lily was a child out of control, and Abigail could not exercise proper parental control over her. The authorities removed Lily from the home; it was unlikely she would return.

He secured legal counsel for Abigail, and also convinced Lily's dad and step-mum to take custody of the unruly teen since Abigail was unlikely to retain it. He had warned Abigail in the past not to permit the child to control her.

"You are her mother; she is not your mother," he said on one occasion. "She is your daughter and not your friend," he said on another. But Abigail had been too weak to enforce proper discipline with Lily.

His phone rang, interrupting his thoughts. It was Mabel, and he smiled. As a single mother, she made him proud. In the short time he was her pastor and mentor, she listened to him and transformed her life. Her academics and business flourished, making her a better woman and mother. Her children were well-behaved, and being around them was always a joy. They were a family that made his burden as a shepherd much lighter.

"Mabel, how are you doing? I apologise for not calling to speak to the girls before bedtime. Is Daisy feeling better now?"

"Good evening, Pastor. We are fine, thank you for asking. And yes, Daisy is feeling better. I'm certain she'll be able to go to school tomorrow."

"God be praised!"

"Hallelujah. Thank you for your prayers, Pastor and for checking on the girls constantly. I can't tell you what a difference your interest in their lives has made."

"I am grateful I can serve God and His people." He paused and waited for her to speak. He sensed her hesitancy. "Is everything okay, Mabel?"

Mabel sighed. "Not quite."

"Talk to me," he encouraged.

"My ex called today."

"He did?" John sounded a little surprised. "But that's a good thing. Isn't it? What did he want?"

"He would like to spend time with the girls over the summer break."

"Well, that's fantastic! Thank you, Lord. I don't see a problem. Surely, you expected him to contact the girls sooner or later."

"Yes, I did. I don't think I am ready to deal with him. I say I have forgiven him, but a part of me still feels bitter."

"Well, don't be bitter, Mabel. Just be better."

Mabel giggled, and John smiled, pleased he made her laugh.

"Okay, Pastor. I'll be better, not bitter."

"Good. That's what I like to hear. Give the man a chance to be a father to his kids. It will do wonders for the girls to have him back in their lives, so ask God for the grace to deal with him. And remember that this is not about you. This is about the girls and what they need. You can't stop their father from seeing them because his presence makes you uncomfortable."

"You're right, Pastor. Thank you for the wise counsel. I'll remember the girls' needs as I navigate my relationship with my ex."

"That's the spirit. Keep me posted on how things go. Good night, Mabel."

"Good night, Pastor John."

***

Victoria lounged on the sofa, her posture relaxed as the vibrant colours and whimsical antics of the cartoon flickering on the television screen captivated her. Laughter from the show echoed around the room, adding a playful energy to the space as she immersed herself in the imaginative world unfolding before her. She heard John's car pull up in front of the house a few minutes ago, but he had yet to come through the front door. Her instinct told her he was on the phone, talking to that dreadful Mabel woman. The woman could do nothing unless she had first spoken to John and was becoming more clingy than all the women in the church put together!

Yesterday, Anna reiterated that a family vacation away from the church and its members was what she and John needed to reconnect with each other. She hadn't yet discussed it with John, but she would be surprised if he joined her and the kids on the trip. The end of the term was fast approaching, and the kids would soon be on summer break, but John had said nothing about whether they would travel as a family.

Victoria frowned, realising John had been in his car for twenty minutes. What was taking him so long? She stormed off the sofa and headed to her bedroom. If he wanted to sit in his car and talk on the phone instead of coming inside to his family, she would not wait up for him another minute. She was going to bed. As she stepped into the dimly lit bedroom, her gaze was instantly drawn to the exquisite lace robe lingerie set draped elegantly across the chair.

The delicate fabric seemed to whisper secrets of allure and seduction. She had gone shopping earlier that day because she was bored and purchased it. The two-piece set comprised a black dressing gown in transparent lacey fabric and a matching thong. It had seemed like a good idea when she'd bought it. She'd never bought anything that daring before. What would be the point?

She eyed the set she had planned to wear tonight and shrugged. What did it matter whether John noticed her or not? What did it matter whether he complimented her? She would dress for herself to make herself happy. She took the set with her into the bathroom as she freshened up for bed. When she resurfaced, she was feeling a little happier and more confident.

She returned downstairs to switch off the television and the lights. John was probably still in his car talking to that blasted woman on the phone. She picked up the remote control to switch off the television. Then she paused and giggled at a funny scene. As she laughed, she thought she heard a key in the door, but she did not turn around, not even as John entered the living room, wrapped his arms around her waist and planted a kiss on her cheek.

"Hello, dear," he greeted. "What are you watching?"

Victoria shrugged without looking at him. "Just a cartoon Paul left on when he turned in for the night," she said. "Can I get you something to eat?"

"No, thanks." He pulled away from her and collapsed into his armchair. "Tom and I stopped at the Thai restaurant near the church to have dinner on our way home."

Victoria nodded as she switched off the television. When they worked late, John and Tom often stopped to grab dinner before going home. With a graceful motion, Victoria leaned down to set the remote control on the polished mahogany coffee table. As she lifted herself upright, she slowly pivoted, her gaze finally settling on John for the first time since he entered the house. He averted his gaze, his fingers deftly working to untangle the knots in his shoelaces as if the task demanded all his focus.

"I've been meaning to tell you. I spoke to Anna a few weeks ago and again yesterday."

He didn't look up. "Oh. How are they doing?"

"They are fine. She's invited us to spend a week with them in the summer. I know how busy you are, but last year, we did not have a family vacation because of your numerous engagements, and I was hoping that this year, we would be able to go away as a family for at least one week."

John shrugged without looking up. "I see no reason why that should be a problem. Booking it for the first week in August should be fine. I have no major engagements that week."

A smile graced Victoria's lips. "I'll book it." She paused as she left the living room, turning to look at him. "Are you coming to bed? You look exhausted."

"Not right away. I need to get some work done in the office."

"Good night, then."

"Good night," he mumbled in response.

As Victoria turned down the sheets and prepared to climb into bed, the bedroom door opened, and John entered, making a beeline for her.

"What are you wearing? I can't concentrate," he said before his lips merged with hers.

What followed next was nothing like what Victoria had ever experienced or expected. At first, he made love to her quickly, as usual. It was always quick, and then he got away from her just as quickly to attend to other business. But this time was different. He held her as he dozed off for a few minutes, and then when he woke up, he made love to her again. This time, it was slow, and it was drawn out. As he slept in the early morning hours, his head nestled against her chest, Victoria wrapped her arms around him. She was hopelessly in love with this man who put everything before her.

As she fell asleep, lovingly stroking his back, his phone vibrated on the bedside table. She could easily see the screen as they slept on his side of the bed. It was

Mabel, and Victoria longed to toss the phone into the toilet. As she moved away from John, he stirred.

"Is that my phone?" he asked groggily.

"Yes." Victoria rolled onto her side, closing her eyes. She had only about two hours before she got up to drive the kids to school. Thankfully, the housekeeper helped them prepare and fed them breakfast. She tuned John out and tried to sleep.

"Hey, Mabel. What's the matter? You sound upset." John pulled the duvet around him and tried to sit up.

"It's Daisy, Pastor John. She's in a lot of pain and feverish. I thought she was getting better, but she's much worse this morning. She didn't sleep too well."

"Calm down, Mabel. Don't panic. Take her to A and E. Is there anyone who can watch Tracy and Stacy?"

"The nanny is due to arrive in an hour."

"Okay. When the nanny arrives, she can help Tracy and Stacy get to school while you take Daisy to A and E."

"Okay, Pastor John. Thank you."

"You're welcome, Mabel. I will call you later to find out how everything's going."

He ended the call and checked the time. It was 6 a.m. He couldn't believe he'd abandoned his work and spent most of the night making love to his wife. What had she been wearing? He shook his head and got out of bed. It was time for a shower, and hopefully, he could get some work done before going into the office.

CHAPTER TEN

Elizabeth entered the house, dropped her suitcases in the hallway, and stretched, placing her hand over her mouth just before a yawn escaped. The price she paid for travelling with Barry was a lack of sleep. During their trips, she usually worked from the hotel suite while he attended his business meetings, and in the evenings, they dined together, partied, and had sex into the early hours of the morning. Since these trips were usually short, the flights long, and the time zones changed, she ended up sleeping very little. And the trips had become frequent. This trip to Dubai was their third trip abroad in the last three weeks.

She entered the kitchen to get some water to drink, relishing the quietness in the house. She had dropped the boys off with Chris on Thursday before her trip. He was due to bring them home later. She wanted to rest before they returned and hoped Chris would give them dinner before bringing them home, as she was too tired to cook. She returned to the hallway and took her cases upstairs to her bedroom. As she walked down the upstairs hall to her room, she noticed that James's door stood open and his room was untidy.

She had not seen it on Thursday morning as they left home. And while her body ached, and she did not want to bother herself with tidying James' room, she couldn't ignore the mess. Groaning, she abandoned her suitcases by her bedroom door and entered James' room to tidy up the mess. He had clothes thrown everywhere: on the bed, on the floor and hanging off the wardrobe doors. It was difficult to tell what was clean and what was not. She couldn't do this. She would need to get a live-in housekeeper.

Chris had not wanted to employ another after the last one quit. He argued that the boys needed their parents and not strangers watching them and the home. She had agreed because he'd been home and looking after the house and the boys. They used a cleaning company a couple of times every week. But as Chris no longer lived here, she would need to employ another housekeeper. She sorted through the clothes, dropping the dirty ones in the laundry basket and the clean ones she folded in a pile to place them in the wardrobe only to discover that the wardrobe was also in a sorry state.

"For heaven's sake, James. When are you going to learn to tidy up after yourself?" she muttered under her breath.

She began to tidy up the wardrobe, putting the clothes and other items where they ought to be. As she worked, she stumbled across a small black leather pouch lying on the wardrobe floor. She frowned as she wondered what it could be. The pouch didn't look like anything James owned. She had certainly never seen it before. She picked it up and opened it. Inside, she found several wraps of a brownish substance. It looked like drugs. Possibly heroin. With trembling hands, she pushed it away from her and watched with wide eyes and her mouth agape as it fell to her feet, exposing a couple of wraps.

What was a pouch with drugs doing in James' closet? Where would this lead? Would her son be arrested for drug possession? Possession with intent to supply? How was this happening? What was James looking for? Money? Her children had everything they needed. They attended an expensive private school, wore designer clothing, and travelled first class. Obviously, she hadn't done enough.

"No. This is not happening to me. This is not happening," Elizabeth cried, running both hands through her hair and ruffling it. "I must speak to John immediately."

She walked briskly out of the room. Her bags were still in the hallway in front of her bedroom. She took her mobile phone from her handbag and dialled John's number.

"John, I need you to come to my house immediately," she said when he answered the phone. "No, John, it cannot wait. Unless you want to officiate my funeral before the week is over." She hung up and began to pace the hall.

John was dining with his family, but Elizabeth had to see him now. His home was a fifteen-minute walk from hers, so she knew he would be ringing her doorbell at any moment. Knowing him, he would not be able to carry on with his meal, not when his sister was distressed.

She was right. The doorbell rang as she made her way down the stairs to the living room. She hurriedly opened it and let him in. John entered the house, put an arm around her shoulder and steered her towards the living room.

"This had better be good, Elizabeth," he warned. "This was one Sunday I hoped to eat dinner with my family, and you called me out. What is the matter?"

Elizabeth took a deep breath, almost as though she needed to muster all her strength for what she was about to say.

"James is on drugs." She finally let out the words.

If she expected her brother to become hysterical, she was bitterly disappointed. He stood towering over her, his hands crossed over his chest on one raised slightly to support his chin.

"I see."

"Well, you seem to be very cool about it!" Elizabeth snapped. "Did you just hear what I said? James, my son, your nephew, your parents' grandson, is on drugs."

John nodded slowly to show that he had heard her the first time, and his pensive look confirmed that he had comprehended the matter. "And you happen to know this how?" he asked calmly.

"Come with me." She took him by the hand and pulled him up the stairs to James' room, where the pouch with the little wraps of brownish substance lay on the carpet. "There!" she pointed triumphantly.

"Elizabeth, all this tells me is that there is a pouch with what might be drugs in it lying on the carpet in James' room," he said.

Elizabeth threw up her hands in exasperation. "What is the matter with you?" she cried. He was acting completely different to how she had expected. "This is serious."

"Calm down. I agree that drugs in my nephew's bedroom is serious. Speaking of which, where is he anyway? Where is the accused person? Why is he not here?"

"He and Andrew went over to Chris for the weekend since I was going to be away."

"Yes, your business trip to Dubai." He nodded. "How did that go, by the way?"

Elizabeth shrugged. She refused to feel guilty for lying and deceiving her brother. It hadn't been a business trip for her. It was a business trip for Barry, who had meetings to attend on Friday and Saturday. She had just accompanied him as she often did when he went abroad. But she had worked from their hotel suite on Friday and Saturday despite being jetlagged so she supposed it could count as a business trip for her as well. She dragged herself back to the present and the conversation with John.

"It was a very short but pleasant and successful trip." Those had been Barry's exact words when she'd asked him how his business concerns had gone before they parted ways at the airport.

"Good. Well, I will be on my way home now." He turned and headed for the stairs.

"What?" Elizabeth looked shocked. "I called you to resolve this issue, John. I need you to do something!"

John paused and turned to her. "Well, I can hardly speak to James if he isn't here, can I?"

"He's at Chris's!"

"Elizabeth, you should have called Chris and asked him to bring the boys home before calling me over."

"You've got a point. I wasn't thinking clearly."

John pursed his lips to refrain from telling her that she was never thinking clearly. He sometimes wondered how she did her job as a lawyer, but her success indicated that her job might be the only place where she thought clearly.

"Ask him to call me when he gets in, and I'll arrange to meet and have a word with him," he said.

Elizabeth sighed in relief. "Thank you, John."

"You're welcome." John descended the stairs with Elizabeth in tow. Just then, the front door opened, and Andrew burst into the house, with James following behind with the cases. Chris stood in the doorway, making no attempt to enter.

Andrew ran to hug Elizabeth, who patted him tenderly on the head. Then he looked up shyly at his uncle. "Good evening, Uncle John."

"Good evening, Andrew. Did you enjoy your weekend with Daddy?" John asked affectionately, and Andrew's enthusiastic nod brought a smile to his face. "Hello, Chris. It was nice to see you in church today."

He had caught a glimpse of Chris in the front row while delivering the message. He knew Chris had only been in because Elizabeth was away, which seemed to be the pattern since he had moved out of the matrimonial home. John made a mental note to make time to visit him and have a word, especially in light of the new revelation concerning James. He had always been concerned about his nephews and thought neither Chris nor Elizabeth was doing enough to ensure their children walked in the ways of the Lord.

Chris smiled without meeting his eyes. "Hello, John; I had no idea you saw me."

"I did. And it will be nice to see you more," he said.

Chris laughed and turned to Elizabeth. "Welcome home. Did you have a good trip?"

"I did, thank you for asking. And thank you for watching the boys. Have they had dinner?"

"Yes!" Andrew enthusiastically announced, rubbing his belly, and everyone laughed—everyone except James, who stood in the corner looking as grumpy and attitudinal as the average teenager.

"Is everything okay, James?" Elizabeth asked.

"What do you care?"

"That is not how to talk to your mother, young man!" John snapped. "And pull your trousers up; I don't want to see your dirty boxers!"

James hurriedly pulled his trousers, which had been riding low on his hips, exposing his boxers with the

Calvin Klein brand name on the waistband. It was his standard way of dressing unless he was in the presence of the man who was both his pastor and uncle, and the disciplinarian called in often by his parents to set him straight. From a young age, he had always experienced unease around his maternal uncle, who always seemed to tower over him and was as quick to rebuke as he was to praise.

"I'm sorry, Pastor, I mean Uncle John."

"And what do you say to your mother?" John asked.

"I'm sorry, Mum."

John nodded. "And what else?"

"Did you have a good trip?"

Smiling, Elizabeth walked over to hug her older son. "I had a good trip, darling. But I missed you." She ruffled his curly afro hair, which was a shade darker than hers, and kissed his cheek.

"I guess I will be on my way now," Chris said.

John turned to him. "I think you should stick around for a little while, Chris. Elizabeth called me because she found drugs in James's bedroom."

A stunned Chris looked from John to Elizabeth and stepped into the house, shutting the door behind him.

James looked shocked and then angry. "Why are you going through my stuff? What did you go into my bedroom for? You're not allowed in my room!"

"Be quiet, young man!" John growled. "You are in much trouble right now."

"James, son, is this true?" Chris asked.

"Is James in trouble?" Andrew asked, looking up at John.

"Yes, he is," John replied, and as Andrew began to cry, he turned to Elizabeth. "I think you should take him upstairs and get him ready for bed. Chris and I will deal with this."

Elizabeth nodded and led Andrew, sobbing, up the stairs toward his bedroom. John turned to look at Chris.

"I think we need to go up to James's bedroom, where the evidence is lying on the floor."

Speechlessly, Chris followed John and James upstairs to James's bedroom, where the pouch with the small wraps of brownish substance was lying on the carpet.

Chris picked it up, opened it and looked at James. "James, what is this doing in your bedroom? Is it yours?"

Chris looked so disappointed that one look at his father's face was enough to break James down.

"I'm sorry, Dad. I didn't mean to disappoint you. Oliver Campbell gave it to me because I wanted to hang out with him and his friends. But I didn't do anything with it, I promise. Some guy was meant to come and get it from me, but he never came, and Oliver said I could hold on to it until I saw him in church again, except I didn't have it with me in church today."

"When did Oliver give it to you?" John asked.

"After the Bible study on Wednesday. He said I had to deliver it to some guy if I wanted to hang out with him and his friends."

"Is this the truth?" John asked. "Because a meeting will be arranged between you, your parents, Oliver, and his parents, and if I find out that you are lying, there will be serious consequences, young man!"

James looked at his father. "I promise you, Dad, I am not lying."

Chris turned to John. "I believe him. Set up the meeting."

Elizabeth walked in just then. "Set up what meeting?"

"James has told us he got the drugs from Oliver Campbell," John said.

"Oliver Campbell?" Elizabeth asked in disbelief. "What is wrong with you, James? How many times have I asked you to stay away from Oliver Campbell?"

"Well, fortunately, James has touched none of the substance, so that's one less thing to worry about," Chris said.

"So he says," John said. "I want to call a meeting with Oliver and his parents; you and Chris will need to attend with James so we can resolve this matter."

"There would be nothing to resolve if my child would do as I say. But no, he has to be stupid and get involved with Oliver Campbell, who every parent in the church knows is a bad influence." She turned to James. "What are you doing with the likes of Oliver Campbell? Why can't you hang around with John Jr. instead? He is well-behaved and always gets excellent grades. Rebekah too. And they are your cousins. Why can't you hang around with them? Why can't you be more like your cousins?"

The question, why can't you be more like your cousins, was one James had heard for as long as he could remember. He didn't see how his mother expected him to be like his perfect cousins when her parenting style was very different to that of her brother. But he could hardly say that here and now, could he? He was in enough trouble as it was. He would be in even bigger trouble if Oliver Campbell knew he had snitched on him. Oliver was a dangerous guy with dangerous friends who would think nothing of stabbing him as he walked down the street. But no one would listen to him except his dad.

"Calm down, Elizabeth. He's made a mistake, and thank God, he hasn't gone far. We can correct this, and I'm sure he's learnt his lesson," Chris said. "You've learnt your lesson, haven't you, buddy?"

"Yes, Dad."

"Good." Chris patted his back.

John looked at Elizabeth and then Chris. "I will inform you when I have set up the meeting."

As John turned to leave, James grabbed his dad's hand. "Oliver will kill me if he knows I told on him."

The desperation in James's voice caused John to stop in his tracks. When he turned, Elizabeth had paled slightly, and Chris looked a little horrified as the import of James's words hit them.

"John, I think this ends here. I will get rid of the drugs," Chris said and turned to James. "Is there more?"

James shook his head. "No, that's it."

"James Dagogo David-West, are you sure?" Elizabeth screamed at him.

"Yes!" He turned to Chris. "That's all he gave me."

"I'll take it with me and get rid of it," Chris said.

"Are you sure this is the best way to handle this?" John asked.

"Yes! I can't afford to take a chance with my son's life. Oliver Campbell may very hurt him if he knows he reported this issue to anyone," Elizabeth said.

"Okay then. This ends here. Chris, get rid of it immediately, and young man, I don't want to hear that you are seen with Oliver Campbell and his likes in the future. Is that understood?"

"Yes, Uncle John."

On that note, John turned and went downstairs with Chris and Elizabeth, who walked him to the front door.

CHAPTER ELEVEN

As her phone beeped, Rebekah paused in the middle of packing her suitcase and reached for it. It was a text from Conor. She sighed and hesitated, wondering if it was a good idea to open and read the message. Their relationship had been a little strained. Conor wanted sex. He'd made that clear from the beginning, and although he'd been willing to wait for her to turn eighteen, the moment she had, he piled on the pressure.

Unfortunately, she couldn't leave home unchaperoned, so he made requests for her to take off her clothes while on video calls with him. The first time she'd succumbed, her brothers had walked in, and John Jr. had reported to their mother, who made her confess her sins and had a serious conversation with her afterwards about the dangers of exposing her nudity online.

They resorted to video calls late at night when she was supposed to be in bed, and no one would enter her room. At first, she enjoyed taking her clothes off for Conor, but he wanted more and asked her to do things that made her uncomfortable and he failed to listen when she explained she wasn't ready. Their fight last night was intense and filled with hurtful words. His unkind remarks about her body left her in tears for most of the night. Feeling a little apprehensive, she opened and read the message.

Forgive me. Last night, I was feeling frustrated. You're travelling today, and we won't be able to chat until you get back. I wanted to resolve our issues before you left.

A smile played on her lips as the message surprised her, and she shot off a text in response.

I forgive you, and I'm sorry, too. I'll be back before you know it. It's only one week, not a lifetime.

His text arrived before she could put her phone down.

It feels like a lifetime. I miss you already. Please don't make me wait any longer. Promise me you'll come to me when you return.

Rebekah let out a sigh. She had previously made it clear she couldn't visit without a chaperone. He had to wait until she started university in September. At university, she'd be without a chaperone and free to leave school and see him.

I need you to wait for me. We talked about this already. My university resumption in September is only six weeks away.

Less than a minute later, he replied.

Okay, my little virgin. I'll wait. You're worth the wait.

Rebekah texted back quickly.

And you promise not to pressure me in the meantime?

She chewed on her bottom lip as she waited for his response. It came almost instantly.

I promise.

A little laugh escaped her lips. She hoped he would keep to his word. Conor was a great guy, but she couldn't stand it when he pressured her. She texted back.

I intend to hold you to your promise. Bye for now. I love you.

I love you too, my beautiful, sexy angel.

Rebekah read the text, a smile playing about her lips, and she tossed her phone away. There was a knock on her door, and her mother looked in, gasping as she saw the state of the room with clothes strewn everywhere.

"Hurry up, Rebekah. The taxi will be here in less than an hour."

Rebekah grinned cheekily. "I am almost ready," she said. "I am just trying to see if I can take everything with me." She pointed to a pile of clothes on the bed.

Victoria rolled her eyes. "Well, you can't, not in that suitcase and certainly not for a one-week trip. So make up your mind already on what goes and what stays. You haven't got all day."

"Yes, Mum," Rebekah flashed another cheeky grin as Victoria left her room.

Victoria walked down the hall and knocked on John Jr.'s door, opening it slightly as she heard prayers emitting from within. John Jr. was already packed and pacing his room, praying in tongues. He smiled at Victoria, pointed to his packed suitcase, and gave her a thumbs-up. Victoria smiled and shut the door behind her.

Her little boy was growing up to be a man of God, as John had prophesied when he was born. She couldn't tell if it was a good thing or a bad thing. While she wanted all her children to love God and serve Him better than she did, she didn't want John Jr. to become his father all over again, building a strong, vibrant spiritual life and serving God's people to the detriment of his immediate family.

She walked down the hall to Paul's room, where he was engaged in a heated argument with Lindsay over what he wanted to take with him on the trip. Victoria paused in the open doorway.

"We're only going for a week, Paul," she reminded him gently. "You'll be back soon enough to play with whatever toys you can't take with you. Do as Lindsay says." She smiled appreciatingly at the long-suffering housekeeper, who was doubtless looking forward to a week's holiday in their absence and walked away.

Her next stop was John. She had packed his bags, but she had to make sure he was ready. He was downstairs in his home office and had been locked in there for the last three hours, making calls and taking care of some last-minute paperwork. She needed to remind him when the cab would arrive, or he would get lost in his work. It had happened the year before last when they had travelled together as a family, and they had almost missed their flight.

John turned in his swivel chair as he spoke to a church member on the phone. "Njeri, the only reason you're in this trouble is because you failed to listen to me when I told you a year ago that this man is a gigolo and you can't marry him. The signs were there; he wasn't the man God had for you, but you cried and talked about your age and the need to marry and have children before you hit menopause."

John paused his movement, sighed, and ran a hand through his hair as Njeri cried. Why did women cry instead of doing what was required of them? Give him a hundred more years on earth, and he would never understand.

"It's okay, Njeri. There's no need to cry. God forgives you for not listening to Him, and now you need to forgive yourself and fix the marriage if it's fixable. Let's talk in a week's time. Come to the office and see me next week. It'll be better to discuss this in person, and we can find a way forward. I'll be praying for you in the meantime. Bye for now."

The door opened, and Victoria peered inside as he ended the call and looked up. John smiled and held out his hand to her. He had a gift for her and couldn't wait to see her reaction when she discovered what it was. As she neared and took his hand, he pulled her onto his lap, secretly smiling at her shocked expression. She was going to be even more surprised when she saw his gift. Without waiting for her to say anything, he framed her face with his large hands and kissed her lips.

"I've got something for you to take on the trip."

Victoria frowned. What could he have for her to take on the trip? She had packed her bags. "What is it?"

Putting her away from him so she was forced to stand, John pulled a large gift bag from under his desk. Victoria saw the name and instantly recognised the bag as coming from an upscale lingerie boutique. She frowned as John placed the bag on the desk and leaned back in his chair.

"What's this?" she asked, taken aback. It was unlike John to buy her a gift when it wasn't a special occasion. Although he readily provided her with money, his busy schedule prevented him from going to the store. He tried on her birthdays and at Christmas but ruined it by dragging Elizabeth to the store or a woman from church with him. Victoria's mood dampened when she thought of her husband going to the store with that horrible woman, Mabel. She doubted it, though. Listening to John's calls and prayers, she concluded that Mabel was preoccupied with her daughter's recent hospital tests. She looked at John, eyebrow raised, expecting him to tell her what was in the bag.

"Why don't you look inside?" John asked, watching her with amusement.

Victoria did as she was told, pulling out several lace robes and matching tongs similar to the kind she had worn the other night. John must have liked it to have bought her some more. She put the items back in the bag and turned to look at him, shrieking as he pulled her onto his lap again.

"What do you think?"

"Did you go alone to buy them?"

"Yes. I couldn't ask anyone to get involved in buying something so intimate." He paused, then added, "I did get some help from the sales ladies in the store, though."

With a laugh, Victoria playfully poked him in the ribs. "I like them, and I can't wait to wear them for you while we're on holiday."

"I will look forward to it—every night. There are seven of them. One for every night we'll be away."

"Look out, Pastor John. You could become carnal."

"That summarises the plan for the next week." He chuckled, cupped her face, and kissed her.

As the kiss intensified, Victoria pulled back and glanced at her Cartier watch. "The cab will be here in about half an hour."

"That's sufficient time for me. I need a few minutes to pray and meditate, and I'm ready."

Victoria rose and grabbed her gift bag. "Okay. I'll call you when the cab is here. I need to pack these."

The cab arrived half an hour later, and Victoria went downstairs, leaving John Jr. to bring down the suitcases.

"Dad's still in his office," she told John Jr. as he brought down the last case and placed it in the foyer. "Tell him the cab has arrived."

"I'm on it." John Jr. walked briskly towards his father's home office.

"I hope he's ready to go and won't make us late like the last time he travelled with us," Rebekah mumbled, and Victoria glared at her, indicating that she should remain silent.

John Jr. returned almost immediately, and a few minutes later, John followed. He was talking on the phone and appeared to be under much pressure. Victoria wondered what the matter was, but she didn't have to wonder for too long, as John soon got off the phone and looked at her. His eyes were grim.

"I can't go, Victoria. I'm sorry."

She looked at him in disbelief, wondering what he was talking about.

"You can't go where?" she asked.

"I can't make the trip. Mabel's youngest daughter received a cancer diagnosis. She needs me. I must go to them now."

Victoria gasped, unable to believe what she was hearing. "Mabel's daughter is ill. How is that our business? Mabel needs you. Where is her husband? There are other pastors in the church. If she needs someone to stand by her now, why you?!"

Victoria stopped talking just as quickly as she'd begun, just as shocked at her outburst as she believed John must be. She had never raised her voice at him in all the years they had been married. Her eyes darted around to their children, who had become statues, no doubt shocked into stillness by their mother's unexpected frenzy.

John looked at her in utter disbelief, and she knew what was going on in his mind. He thought she didn't care about the woman whose child was terminally ill, but that was far from the truth. She cared, but she wanted to be with her husband alone for one week without disruption. Was that too much to ask?

"Victoria?" John was too shocked to know what else to say.

Victoria held up a hand to stop him from saying anything more. "Go, Pastor John. Go to her. You're right. She needs you. Go."

John walked through the foyer, ignoring his family and the packed suitcases lining the hall, and out of the house, shutting the door behind him. Victoria pulled herself together, not wanting the children to see how devastated she was. She looked at all three children and forced a smile.

"Where's Dad gone?" Rebekah asked, like she could not believe what had just transpired.

"Are you deaf?" John Jr. unleashed his anger on her. "Didn't you just hear him say–?"

"John Jr., you will not speak to your sister that way!" Victoria snapped.

"I'm sorry," he mumbled.

"Thanks, Mum." Rebekah smiled at her mother and then scowled at her brother.

"Dad's had an emergency, so he's not going," Victoria announced, looking at all three children.

"Maybe he can come later?" Paul asked hopefully.

Victoria smiled and patted her youngest on the head. "I doubt that, Paul."

"Are we not going then, Mum?" Paul looked sad.

Just then, the doorbell rang, and John Jr. went to answer it. When he returned, he announced, "It's the cab driver, Mum. He's getting impatient."

"What do we do now, Mum?" Rebekah asked. "Surely we can't go without Dad."

"Did Dad say we could still go?" Paul asked.

Victoria looked on, unable to answer and unsure of what to do next. Suddenly, John Jr. took charge of the situation.

"Dad's made his choice. He's not going. We need to make our choice whether we go or stay. I don't know about the rest of you, but I've got my ticket, so I'm going." Without another word, he took his case and moved towards the door.

Rebekah followed him behind. "Me too."

Paul shrugged and followed her closely behind. "Me three."

Victoria watched her three children leave the house. Cancelling what could still be a good trip was pointless. Some time with her mother, sister, and niece would be a treat for her. John wasn't necessary for her to enjoy this holiday.

CHAPTER TWELVE

Barry pulled up in front of Mabel's home, bringing his Porsche Cayenne to a halt beside her Audi Q6. He had mixed feelings as he sat in the car and took in his surroundings. It was his first time in Mabel's home, and he wished the occasion was a happier one that allowed him to appreciate the beautiful neighbourhood and the two-storey white house, its red and yellow brick-tiled driveway, manicured lawn, and flowerbeds he could glimpse through the side gate leading to the back garden.

Mabel had not exactly invited him here today, although she had permitted it as she'd been in the background as he spoke to Tracy. He recalled her saying, "Yes, you can tell Dad. I need to call Pastor John."

The news had not been one he'd been expecting; it shook him to his very foundation. He was gripped by a dread he hadn't known for years. His immediate concern had been for Mabel and how she was coping. They had not interacted much after their first call weeks ago, his calls mainly being with the girls, but he'd found himself eager to speak to her, hear her voice in the background, and look at the pictures that Steve constantly sent him.

Now, he found himself wanting to hold her and comfort her.

Mabel opened the door as he rang the bell, and he let his gaze run over her, taking in her wide-leg jean trousers and Ankara wrap-top with long sleeves that flared at the wrists. He had seen a similar design on *Ara's* website. He had been observing her business with the same keen interest that he observed her social media posts. His obsession was unbelievable. He experienced distress seeing her red, tear-filled eyes. As he stepped into the house, he reached out to pull her into his arms to comfort her, but she stepped back and out of his reach.

"Daisy's lying on the sofa in the living room," she informed him, looking away and wiping a tear as she shut the door.

Barry nodded as he studied closely. When it became clear that she wouldn't look at him, speak to him, or allow him to comfort her, he turned and walked through the hall into the living room. A glance around the room indicated that Mabel had tried to move on without him. There wasn't a single furnishing that he remembered from their old home in Manchester, and as he glanced from the mantelpiece to the display cabinet and the walls, he saw none of their old family photos.

All the photos were new and taken following his departure. Mabel had wasted no time embracing her life as a single mother. No doubt, without plenty of help from the good pastor. He refused to contemplate that and let his gaze fall on Daisy, who lay on the elegant U-shape sofa with its generously sized back cushions and multiple scatter cushions. A throw was spread across her little body, and her gaze was captivated by the colourful animation flickering on the television screen, drawing her into a world of whimsical characters and exciting adventures.

She looked tired and sleepy, and Barry experienced a heart-stopping moment; he couldn't move. His little girl was ill, and there wasn't a thing he could do about it. He experienced complete helplessness and uselessness as he drew closer and sat on the edge of the sofa next to her, taking her frail body in his arms. She had lost considerable weight, but he was thankful to hold her close and enjoy the warmth of her body.

The last couple of weeks had been challenging for the little one as she had been in and out of hospitals as tests were run to determine what was wrong with her. Mabel received the test results this afternoon, and all hell had broken loose. Daisy had been diagnosed with leukaemia. His little girl had cancer. After Tracy's call, he had left everything and cancelled all his meetings to rush to her side. It was scary and unbelievable. He reflected on the one year he had been away, an entire year he had missed in the life of his little girl and in the lives of all his daughters. Time he would not get back, and now it seemed fate had decided his time with Daisy would be even shorter than he thought.

On his way here, he'd been praying to God, pouring out his heart. Desperate for his daughter's health, he cried and made promises. If God would heal Daisy and not let her die, he would do everything to get back his family and be a good father and husband. He would become a serious

Christian, committing his time and money to God's service. Leaving Mabel and the girls had been a mistake, but he didn't want to get them back, only to bury his little girl.

As he held her tightly, he prayed again. His little girl did not deserve to have her life cut short.

Lord, if this is payback for my sins, please have mercy, and if you must take anyone, please take me, and leave my little girl, he begged.

"Daddy, are you crying?" Daisy asked as she pulled back to look at her father's tear-soaked face.

She framed his face and wiped his tears. "I will be okay, Daddy," she assured him. "Pastor John will come and pray for me, and I will be healed."

The doorbell rang, and Mabel, who had been pacing in the hallway, rushed towards the front door. "That must be Pastor John."

She opened the front door, and relief washed over her when she saw John standing on the other side. As soon as he crossed the threshold of the house, she threw herself into his embrace, her emotions overwhelming her. Tears streamed down her cheeks, a flood of both anguish and relief spilling forth as she clung to him tightly.

"Oh, Pastor John, I'm so glad you're here. I am so devastated. My little girl. My poor, poor little girl. Why her? Why me?"

"Calm down, Mabel, calm down. Daisy will be fine. I need you to have faith and to believe the report of the Lord above the report of the doctor."

Mabel pulled away and looked up at him. "I'm trying, Pastor John, but this is so difficult. I am watching my baby die before my eyes. The doctors want to start chemotherapy right away."

John tucked his Bible under his arm and, with his right hand free, placed a finger over Mabel's lips to silence her.

"Mabel, I need you to watch what you say and to speak from a place of faith and not a place of fear. No one is dying. The doctor has said that Daisy has cancer; that may or may not be correct. And even if that is correct, that is only a fact and not the truth. The truth is that Daisy's infirmities have been taken away by the Lord, and by His stripes, she was healed over two thousand years ago. God's word is powerful and works for a headache as much as it works for cancer. The question is, do you believe?"

Mabel gazed up at him in awe. This man never ceased to amaze her; he always had an answer for everything and offered a comforting word in every crisis. She was feeling better already.

As she gazed intently at him, John slipped his arm around her shoulder, drawing her closer. "It is going to be okay, Mabel. I have never known God to fail. But you need to believe. Only believe."

Barry Babs-Jonah laid Daisy against the cushions as he stood up, furrowing his brows as he took in the sight before him. He gazed at Mabel, nestled in the embrace of the man he recognised as her pastor, whom he had seen in countless pictures with her on social media, and a surge of anger coursed through him.

He didn't want to annoy God after asking for His help, and he knew he had no claim on Mabel as she was no longer his wife, but seeing her leaning on the other man for comfort made him want to punch something. Mabel and the girls may think the sun rose and set with Pastor John and that he could not do anything wrong, but Barry knew there was no such reality as a perfect human being. He cleared his throat, causing Mabel to remember his presence.

"Barry, this is Pastor John of The Vine Church," Mabel said, pulling out of John's arms and looking at Barry. "Pastor John, this is Barry Babs-Jonah, the girls' father."

The girls' father. That was what he had reduced himself to.

Mabel's introduction couldn't have made it any clearer that his presence was tolerated only because of the girls. Barry extended his hand to shake John's. As their hands met in a firm grip, both men took a moment to assess one another, noting their similar height and build. The air crackled with a sense of rivalry as they exchanged measuring glances, each sizing up the other with a mixture of apprehension and anticipation.

John looked at Barry, trying to understand what kind of man abandoned his wife and kids. Barry looked at John, trying to figure out what kind of man gave so much time to other families. What time did he have for his? Neither man was impressed with the other. Barry made a mental note to ask his assistant to get him the man's messages. He would listen and decipher what kind of preacher he was. If the man was no good, he intended to protect Mabel and the girls from him.

"It's a pleasure to meet you, Pastor John."

"It's a pleasure to meet you too, Mr Babs-Jonah." John released Barry's hand and looked at Mabel. "I'm going to pray with Daisy and be on my way. And I suggest you run another test. Keep me posted on what happens."

"Do you mean get a second opinion?" Barry asked.

John shrugged. "Call it getting a second opinion or getting confirmation that God has healed her. But go again after I pray today."

Barry narrowed his eyes to slits. He would have to keep a close eye on this smooth-talking pastor. The man sounded too confident and too smooth talking to be up to any good. John held his gaze briefly before turning to Mabel.

"Where are Tracy and Stacy?"

"They're upstairs in their bedrooms. They were a little distraught when I shared the news with them, so it's probably best they stay there as Daisy is drifting in and out of sleep, and I don't want them disturbing her with their crying."

"God will turn your sorrows into joy. He's able," John said. "Do you believe?"

The question was directed at Mabel, who vigorously nodded her head. Barry continued watching John with narrowed eyes. He would let the man of God have his moment, and then Daisy would be subjected to another round of tests. If nothing changed, God help the man of God.

John ignored Barry as he approached Daisy. He placed his Bible and anointing oil on the coffee table and leaned over the sleepy child, putting his hand on her temple.

"How are you feeling, Daisy?" he asked.

"Tired, but I will be better when you pray, Pastor John."

A smile spread across John's face. "Your faith is incredible, little one."

He straightened, opened up his Bible and read several healing scriptures. When he was done, he shut the Bible and looked at Barry and Mabel. "God's word is quick. God's word is powerful. You only need to believe."

Placing his hand on Daisy's head again, he rebuked the foul spirit of infirmity, asking it to come out, depart, and never return. When he was done, he anointed her. "By the power of the Holy Ghost, your healing is sealed, in the name of Jesus."

"Amen!" Mabel declared enthusiastically. Daisy had dropped off to sleep and was snoring gently. Mabel tucked the throw around her more snuggly and kissed her cheek before turning to John. "Thank you so much, Pastor John."

"All the thanks go to Jesus, Mabel. I am only a vessel." John picked up his Bible and anointing oil. "I will leave you now and await your good news."

"Goodbye, Pastor John." Barry slipped his hands into the pockets of his business suit to avoid shaking hands again.

"Goodbye Mr Babs-Jonah." John spared him only a glance before looking at Mabel. "Walk me to my car, Mabel."

Mabel linked her arm through John's and walked with him towards the front door, chatting animatedly. Barry's jaw clenched tightly as he watched them walk away, frustration bubbling inside him as he recalled she had flirted with him similarly in the blissful early days before they were married.

As John drove home, he thought about his family, who would no doubt be on their way to the airport, and his heart sank. This wasn't how he wished things to be. He wanted to make the trip, but Mabel needed him, and even now, he would stick around and provide what support she needed as she took Daisy in for another round of tests. Would Victoria understand? Her outburst earlier had been unprecedented.

"God help me," he muttered under his breath. He pulled off the road briefly and called Liam. "Liam, please see if you can order a new Mercedes for Victoria. I want it delivered as soon as possible. It should be the same version as what she has now but this year's model."

Liam was silent at the other end of the line, no doubt wondering about this request. Liam knew he was not a man given to impulse buying and planned his expenditures. He would have hinted at Liam a few months before for something like this.

"Did you hear me?"

"Yes, I did, Pastor John; I'll take care of it immediately."

"Good man."

John ended the call and pulled his car back on the road. It was a small price to pay to make Victoria happy. She liked Mercedes cars, especially the version she had. It was now three years old. She had asked for a new one months ago, and he had ignored her. Buying it now would smooth things over, as he had failed to make the trip with her.

He prayed that when it arrived, she would see it as the peace offering that it was and not give him hell.

CHAPTER THIRTEEN

John wadded the paper into a ball and tossed it into the bin across his desk, chuckling as it landed perfectly inside. He was quite impressed with his throw, but as he gazed at his computer screen again, he frowned and rubbed his forehead. His early departure from the church to work alone in the quiet of his home office did not improve his concentration.

His family was due back from their one-week vacation in Texas the following day, and he was somewhat distracted. He had not spoken much to Victoria as he had been busy, and most of the time he called, she and the kids were involved in some activity that either made it impossible for them to talk or made their conversation brief.

He sensed it was so because Victoria wanted it that way. The few times they had spoken, she had been in a hurry to get off the phone and nothing had been said about his inability to make the trip with his family. He didn't know what to expect from her when she returned home tomorrow, and that bothered him. Thankfully, her new car was expected to arrive in a few days, and he hoped that it would sweeten her mood.

He looked up from his computer screen and ended his reverie as Lindsay opened the door to his office and peered inside. Ever faithful and dependable, Lindsay should have had some time off when the family travelled but had chosen to remain and serve him once it was apparent he wouldn't be travelling. He made a mental note to ask Victoria to give her a bonus this month and arrange a time for her to take a much-needed holiday.

"Pastor John, there's a lady from the church here to see you; she says her name is Mabel."

Smiling, John pushed back his swivel chair and stood. "Please send her in, Lindsay. Thank you."

He was not expecting to see her, and she had not called to say she was coming. But he was always glad to see Mabel and willing to accommodate her. He also hoped to hear some news concerning Daisy. A moment later, Mabel walked in, beaming and carrying a huge picnic basket. He cast her an appreciative glance as he approached and took the basket from her.

She looked radiant in a knee-length fit and flare Ankara shirt dress from *Ara* featuring giant bell sleeves that flared out from her elbows. She was making so much progress with her clothing line, and he was delighted to see how, with each passing day, she moved away from the woman she'd been when he first met her and transitioned into the woman God wanted her to be.

"Good evening, Pastor John."

"Good evening, Mabel." John set the basket on the desk. "You look beautiful, as always. The dress is from *Ara*?"

"Indeed, it is." She turned around, arms spread out so he could fully appreciate the beautiful design.

John nodded in appreciation. "Your designs are fantastic," he said. "How are you? I certainly was not expecting to see you."

Mabel had been on her way to his office to surprise him with a home-cooked African meal, as she knew his family was away. However, she called Liam to confirm he was in the office and Liam informed her he was working from home. Had his family been around, she would not have come as she tried to stay away from his unfriendly wife. But as she knew he was home alone, she decided to visit.

Her smile was subtle. The corners of her mouth curved slightly upward, and there was a playful glint in her eyes. "I came to feed you."

John peeked inside the basket. Whatever was in it smelt divine. "What have you got in here?"

"There's jollof rice, coconut rice, goat meat stew and fried plantains."

"Yummy. I can't wait to feast on it. You're going to overfeed me at this rate, Mabel," he teased.

She laughed. "It's my way of thanking you for coming to see Daisy the other day."

"It looks like you've gone to much trouble to thank me." He pointed at the basket.

"Oh, no. It was no trouble at all, Pastor John. I love cooking for you."

"You're always very thoughtful and kind, Mabel. Thank you." He indicated an armchair across the desk. "Please, sit down."

"Thank you." Mabel sat and crossed her legs while looking around. "You've got a very beautiful home office, Pastor John."

John looked around the room and nodded in agreement. "Victoria designed it; she thought if I spent a lot of time in here, I might as well be comfortable." He picked up his phone and called Lindsay to his office. She appeared almost immediately.

"Lindsay, please take this basket away, unpack the food, and bring the basket back to Mabel before she leaves."

"Yes, Pastor John." Lindsay removed the basket from the desk and exited as quietly as she entered.

"Thank you for all you have done for the kids and me. In response to your advice to seek a second opinion for Daisy, Barry and I saw a different physician. Blood tests and bone marrow tests showed she was cancer-free. A further test was done, and we're waiting for the results, but I'm certain it will return with no trace of cancer. Daisy has been doing much better since you prayed with her. All complaints of joint pains are gone, and she isn't so tired or feverish anymore. It's so wonderful to watch her play again. I can't thank you enough, Pastor John."

John nodded. "God has done it all. And all the thanks and praise go to Him alone. Bring her to see me after service on Sunday, and I'll anoint her again. What the Lord has done shall be forever."

"Amen," Mabel said. "I will do just that, Pastor John."

"How are things with you and Barry at the moment?" John asked. "He seems to have become more involved with the girls, especially with Daisy's recent health challenge."

"Yes, he has."

"You don't sound very excited."

"I am excited for the girls."

"But not for you?" John asked.

Mabel shook her head. "I'm happy for him to have as much access to the girls as possible. I can't decide if I want him back."

"Has he suggested he might want to return to you?"

"He hasn't exactly said the words, but I can sense that he will say something sooner or later."

"Well, if he hasn't said anything, you don't know anything. Just take each day as it comes. He may want to partner with you to parent the girls."

"Possibly." Mabel shrugged.

The door opened, and Lindsay entered with Mabel's basket.

"Thank you, Lindsay," John said as the other woman put the basket down and retreated, shutting the door behind her.

"Well, I should be on my way home now. Barry is taking the girls out to dinner, and I'm tagging along, so I need to prepare."

As she stood, John got up, walked around his desk, and stood before her, his hands shoved deep inside his trouser pockets. "Thank you once again for the meal, Mabel. I'm certain I will enjoy it."

He stood close, and a shiver ran down Mabel's body as she considered what it would be like if she took a step, then another, and entered his personal space, where her body would brush against his ever so slightly. His white shirt sleeves were rolled up, and he had undone two buttons after taking off his tie. What would he do if she put her hands on that hard chest as she'd been wanting to do for some time? How would he react if she opened two more buttons to get a better view of his chest?

A flutter in her stomach accompanied her upward glance, meeting his eyes; her lips instinctively pressed together, a mix of shyness and intrigue swirling within her. Her eyes locked onto his, and in that moment of intense connection, she sensed his fascination. With newfound courage coursing through her, she stepped boldly forward, closing the distance between them. With a gentle grace, she lifted her hand and brushed her fingers softly against the curve of his face.

"You do so much for me. So much for everyone. Let me look after you for a moment." Gently, she moved her hand into his hair. Holding his gaze, she massaged his scalp with the tips of her fingers.

John closed his eyes, taking a deep breath as waves of tingling sensations coursed through his body, enveloping him in a warm embrace of electrifying energy. But, as Mabel's lips brushed against his, his eyes flew open, and he recoiled, removed her hands from him and stepped back.

"What are you doing?" he demanded.

Mabel lowered her eyes as embarrassment consumed her. Never had a man turned her away with such cutting severity, leaving her heart aching and her pride in tatters. "I am sorry, I thought–"

"Thought what?" he asked, but didn't wait for a response. "Mabel, I'm a married man, and I love my wife very much. Besides, I love the Lord, and His love constrains me. Do you understand?"

"Pastor John, please accept my apologies; I did not intend to offend. You've been there for me, the husband I hoped for and never had, the father I wished for my daughters. Loving and wanting you was inevitable. Won't you allow me to take care of you?"

John shook his head. "My well-being is not your responsibility. Everything I did, I did for the love of Christ. I belong to another and can't be yours, and your feelings aren't divine; your actions contradict God's word.

"I realise this, Pastor John, and I'm sorry." Overwhelmed by her emotions, Mabel's composure shattered, and tears soon engulfed her. "Please pardon me. Don't leave us because of my mistakes, please. It would break the girls if you did. It would break me."

John sighed, pulling her into his arms as she cried. The events that had just transpired left him confused, prompting a period of contemplation. Mabel was attracted to him, and he should have anticipated that. It had happened in the past; his participation in their lives, particularly during tough times, drew women to him. Others had made romantic advances towards him. Yet, Mabel's progress today surpassed everyone else's. Therefore, the problem lay with him, and he must consider why he permitted Mabel's advances before rejecting them.

"I never thought of abandoning you or the girls, Mabel. But I need to correct you. You can't entertain such feelings. It is wrong. Do you understand?"

Mabel nodded and muttered her thanks as John released her and handed her some Kleenex from his desk. She dried her eyes, and at the sound of a soft knock on the door, she jumped and put some space between herself and John.

"Yes, Lindsay?" John looked unperturbed as the housekeeper looked in.

"Mrs Audrey Campbell is here to see you, Pastor," she announced.

"Please send her right in."

He summoned Audrey for a meeting concerning Oliver. During last week's midweek Bible study, someone called the attention of the church security to the smell of marijuana emitting from a stall in the men's bathroom. The youth pastor and the head of security had worked together asking questions of the young people in church and looking at the CCTV footage.

Yesterday, they went to Pastor Tom with their suspicions, and Tom informed him that Oliver Campbell might be recruiting drug sellers within the church. It was only a suspicion based on what people said off-record and what could be inferred from the footage. But they both agreed he should speak with Audrey; hence, he invited her here today.

On hearing Lindsay's announcement, Mabel hurriedly composed herself and threw the used Kleenex in the bin. Just as she picked up her handbag and picnic basket, Audrey Campbell appeared in the doorway, looking radiant in a pair of blue wide-leg jeans trousers and a red V-neck pleated blouse.

"Good evening, Pastor John," Audrey greeted as she stepped into the room and stepped to one side to allow Mabel to exit. "I know you from church. Hello. I am Audrey Campbell."

Mabel accepted the offered handshake. "I know who you are. You're the women leader. My name is Mabel. Mabel Babs-Jonah."

"Lovely to make your acquaintance, Mabel. And I look forward to interacting with you more in church. It would be nice to have a woman like you on my team to help encourage other women."

"What an excellent idea, Audrey. I think it's time you took Mabel under your wing and helped her get settled in the church family," John said.

Mabel glanced at him quickly, but his eyes showed no malice. She smiled and turned to Audrey. "Of course, Audrey." She looked at John again. "Bye, Pastor."

Audrey watched the younger woman intently as she hurried from the room.

A femme fatale, she thought to herself. *She's trouble.*

She turned to give her attention to John, smiling broadly as she noticed he was watching her closely.

"You wanted to see me, Pastor," she reminded him as she moved further into the room.

"Yes, Audrey. Please sit down. I need to have a quick word with you."

"Of course, Pastor John." Audrey sat down and placed her large bucket handbag on the floor beside her.

"It's about Oliver," John said as he returned to his swivel chair and sat down.

Audrey frowned. "What about him?"

"There are allegations he is recruiting young boys in church to sell drugs."

"Oliver?" Audrey looked horrified. "My Oliver would never do drugs, Pastor John. I appreciate he's been in one trouble or the other in the past, but drugs? Never!"

John observed the woman before him intently. As a parent, he could understand her need to defend her son, but it was important that he made her understand that if his findings were true, Oliver might be imprisoned for a long time. He tried to take Oliver under his wing and mentor him, but it never worked. Audrey was a good woman who loved the Lord; she was an excellent women leader, but she left much to be desired as a parent.

"Are you certain of this, Audrey?"

"I am, Pastor John. There must be some mistake."

John sighed. He hoped she was right, and it was a mistake. "Okay. I am going to ask you to have a word with him. And beyond that, I need you to watch his activities when he comes to church. You don't want to be inside the church worshipping, and your son is outside getting arrested."

"God forbid, Pastor John. God forbid." Audrey looked shaken. "I will talk with Oliver as soon as I get home."

John nodded. "You do that, Audrey."

CHAPTER FOURTEEN

Mabel ate her meal quietly and listened as the girls chatted to their dad about school and especially the prizes they had won on prize-giving day. They had not had a chance to discuss properly with their father on the phone since the term ended, as Daisy's cancer diagnosis had taken priority.

But with the diagnosis result changed and Daisy feeling much better, they could now talk about other things. As their father was present and not over the phone, they had the opportunity to express themselves properly, and Barry humoured them, nodding, smiling, and even putting down his cutlery to applaud as the occasion demanded.

She couldn't help but smile. Their achievements had pleased them. Unlike the previous year when only Daisy had won a prize, this year, all three girls won prizes. Daisy had been in pain, having been in hospital the day before to run some tests, but she had walked up the stage with a big smile to collect her prize. Pastor John's children had again cleared most of the prizes. Mabel had spotted Victoria Griffith in a front-row seat, smiling, clapping, and taking pictures.

"Daddy is sorry he was away on business and couldn't attend," Barry said.

Daisy leaned forward and patted his hand. "It's okay, Daddy. Mummy was there. And we liked the dolls you got us from China. They're pretty but not much fun to play with."

"They're not meant for playing." Stacy sounded exasperated. "They're vintage China dolls for display."

Daisy scowled at her. "I don't want a doll for display. I want a doll to bathe and dress and feed!"

Barry threw back his head and laughed, drawing attention from other diners in the exquisite African restaurant. "Okay, Daisy, Daddy's noted the feedback. I'll take you shopping tomorrow, and you can pick the dolls you want."

"Can I come too, Daddy?" Tracy asked.

Barry turned to his eldest, who was seated to his right and stroked her cheek. "Of course you can, sweet cakes." He smiled at Stacy as he turned. "And you too, Stace."

"Thank you, Daddy!" Stacy beamed. "Let's go to the Disney store."

"Yes, let's!" Daisy sounded enthusiastic. "And let's go to Toys R Us!"

"Absolutely!" Barry agreed and sipped his wine. "Tomorrow is for spoiling Daddy's girls. We'll go anywhere you want to go. And while we're on the topic of spoiling Daddy's girls, where do you girls want to go for summer vacation?"

Tracy shrugged as she played with the food on her plate. She was not big on holidays because flying terrified her. "I am happy to stay home like we did last year," she said.

Last year, they had not travelled because Barry had left suddenly, and Mabel had been trying to settle into their new life in London. Barry's sudden departure and relocating to London from Manchester shortly after had all been a lot to deal with in a short time, so when summer came, she couldn't be asked to pack a bag and make a trip. She very much wanted to stay put.

"We had a good holiday last year when we moved to London," Stacy said. "Pastor John took us to loads of places. We went on a rented bus with other kids from church."

"Really?" Barry tried to sound excited, although he was getting tired of hearing all the wonderful things the girls had to say about Pastor John. He had got the man's messages and intended to start listening to them immediately. Pastor John couldn't be as wonderful as he sounded, although Daisy had been healed as he had said. But Barry reasoned that probably had to do with his own prayer.

"Yes, and we had lots of fun," Daisy added excitedly. "We ate loads of ice cream and cake and candy, and we went on the London Eye and to Madame Tussauds and Shrek's Adventure and many other places."

"I'm glad you had a lot of fun," Barry said. "We can go anywhere you want this year, at home in London or abroad. All you have to do is say it."

"Can we go to Disney Land?" Daisy asked.

"Sure, baby."

"We went to Disney two years ago!" Tracy protested.

"That was Disney Florida," Daisy said. "We've never been to Disney Paris. Can we go to Disney Land in Paris, Daddy?"

Barry looked at Tracy, his eyes pleading with her to be agreeable. When Tracy smiled, he turned to Daisy. "Anywhere you want to go, kitten, Daddy will take you."

"Will Mummy come too?"

At Daisy's question, Mabel raised her head and dragged herself out of her thoughts. It was on the tip of her tongue to say she would not be going on vacation with Barry and the girls, but Barry beat her to it. "Of course, Mummy will come too."

Barry looked at Mabel, his eyes daring her to say otherwise. She had been very quiet and withdrawn since he picked her and the girls up earlier this evening for their celebratory dinner. She looked very beautiful in her silver asymmetric one-shoulder mini dress, which revealed square shoulders and nicely toned arms and legs. Her silver strappy stiletto sandals added height to her stature and elegance to her steps. She wore her long-braided hair in a pile on top of her head, with the rest of it falling to her waist.

He'd been unable to stop watching her and even as he conversed with the girls, he observed her closely, evaluating her and thinking how much she had changed, from her clothes to her behaviour. She exuded class and was more confident as she walked through the restaurant frequented by high-net-worth Africans living in London. Gone was the timid woman he had married.

He thought about all the places he would like to take Mabel and the experiences he would like to give her. Perhaps they could take a trip alone without the girls and make love for hours without fear of being interrupted by the kids. He would like that. His body stirred, and he shifted in his chair.

Mabel looked away, unable to hold his gaze, and she picked up her water glass and sipped. If Barry wanted to take the girls away on holiday, it would be best for her to go, wouldn't it? Having made a fool of herself with Pastor John, it was probably best she limited her time around him in the future.

She had yet to stop thinking about the incident without cringing. It was also time to reflect on whether she needed Pastor John now as much as she had when Barry first abandoned her and the girls. Barry was here and wanted to be a father to the girls, and he wasn't leaving her out, so maybe she was probably better off spending her time with him and the girls.

She put down her water glass and smiled at Daisy. "Yes, Mummy will come too."

"Yay!" the girls chorused in unison, and she laughed, delighted at their obvious pleasure.

Her laughter ceased as her gaze shifted to Barry and she noticed him observing her through narrowed eyes. She knew that look. It was a look she had seen many times in her marriage. It was a silent promise of a lovemaking that would blow her mind. Suddenly, she felt warm all over. Her body wanted it, but her head warned her to tread cautiously. She could not afford for him to reject her again when she had not fully recovered from his initial rejection.

After dinner, as they walked out of the restaurant towards Barry's car in the car park, the girls insisted on going to Barry's house before going home.

"We want to see Daddy's new house!" Stacy and Daisy chorused excitedly. Flanking their father, they held his hands, swinging them as they strolled toward the car.

Tracy and Mabel followed behind at a much slower pace, arms around each other's waists.

Barry looked at her as they reached the car. "Is it okay? It will only be for an hour or two. And besides, they're on holiday."

"Okay. One hour or two." Mabel didn't want to dampen the girls' mood.

"Yay! Thank you, Mummy!" Daisy ran to her side and hugged her before letting her father help her onto her booster seat in the rear of the vehicle and secure her seat belt.

Even Tracy and Stacy were grinning ear-to-ear as they climbed in the rear of the vehicle, excited at the prospect of going to their dad's house. Mabel was glad that she had said yes. Their smiles were captivating and tugged at her heart. The girls had missed their dad terribly, and she promised herself she would not get in the way as Barry tried to make amends and spend more time with his daughters.

"Off we go then, Daddy!" Stacy said once everyone was in the vehicle and Barry had got behind the wheel.

Barry chuckled. "Okay. Off we go." He started the engine and drove from the restaurant's car park onto the main road.

Barry's home was beautiful. An architectural masterpiece with more glass than bricks. Mabel wasn't surprised; he had always liked the finer things in life. The girls were thrilled as he took them around the five-bedroom house. She wondered why he had bought such a big house when he lived alone. She saw no sign of a woman or another family as they moved through the large, exquisitely furnished house that looked more like a museum with expensive furnishings than a home.

There wasn't even a sign of a live-in housekeeper. Barry liked his privacy, so Mabel thought he was likelier to have a live-out housekeeper who came in a few times a week to keep everything spotlessly clean. It was very lovely but not for a family with small children. The tour ended in the kitchen with its white marble countertops and floor and expensive-looking gadgets, which looked like they were there more for a show of wealth as she couldn't imagine Barry had the time to do any kind of cooking.

The girls were offered ice cream and cake, and as they sat around the kitchen dining area, Barry switched the television on so they could watch a children's show. Then he led Mabel out through the glass door leading to the back garden and up a flight of stairs to the rooftop, with its beautiful outdoor furnishings and breathtaking view. He walked towards the drinks cabinet and poured her a glass of Baileys Irish cream, to her surprise and delight.

"It used to be your favourite and the only way to get you to drink alcohol," he said as he held out the glass to her.

Mabel smiled as she collected the glass from him. "You remember."

He looked her in the eye. "I remember everything about you."

Mabel looked away, unsure how to respond to that. "Your home is beautiful." She turned her back on him and admired the view before her.

"Yes. I think so, too." Barry watched her as he poured himself a brandy and took a sip. "It's a little too big for one person, though."

Mabel glanced at him momentarily as he walked up to her. "Yes. So I noticed. But why did you buy it?"

He shrugged. "I expected to remarry." It was the truth. When he returned Mabel's bride price, he thought he would find a beautiful woman from Lagos who would be perfect for him, but he did not. The women he was introduced to were only interested in his money and ready to do anything to get it. Their desperation put him off.

Mabel nodded, not sure she could trust herself to speak. Of course, he expected to remarry. He would not have returned her bride price unless he intended to remarry. She stiffened as Barry put an arm around her and encircled her waist, pulling her against him.

"Spend the night."

Mabel gasped at his request and his boldness. She tried to step away from him, but his arm was like a vice around her.

"Say yes. Please."

She shook her head. "No. Absolutely not."

He loosened his hold, and she quickly stepped back, urgently gulping down her drink as if it could wash away the tension in the air. She must be mad. For a moment there, she wanted to say yes. The feel of his body against hers had brought back so many memories of the nights of passion, especially in the early years of their marriage.

"There isn't anyone, Mabel."

"Regardless. We're not married."

"That didn't stop you before."

Mabel looked away as she recalled the night Barry had taken her virginity and the months of sex before her bride price had been paid, and they were officially husband and wife according to the Yoruba native law and customs.

"Things are different now," she said. "Can we talk about something else?"

"You've changed a great deal. And I mean that in a good way. What you've achieved with your body and your mind is phenomenal. I'm impressed."

Mabel nodded. "I am glad you think so. But I didn't do it to impress you."

Barry sipped his brandy and grinned. "Of course. I would like to think that everything you've achieved, you did for yourself."

"Thank you. I like the woman I've become. Pastor John helped me see what was possible, and after that, there was no turning back."

Barry's hand tightened around his glass. Couldn't he have a simple conversation with Mabel and the girls without hearing that man's name? His phone buzzed softly in his trouser pocket, and he pulled it out and frowned as he recognised it was Elizabeth calling.

What did she want?

He cut the call, and he switched off his phone. It was time to end their affair, and he made a mental note to see her soon and do just that. As he put the phone back in his pocket, he realised Mabel was watching him.

"Problems?"

He shrugged. "Business problems," he said. "But nothing that can't be resolved with a quick meeting."

She nodded. "I never could wrap my head around your business while we were married. But as I run *Ara* daily, it's beginning to make sense. *Ara* isn't as big as your African food export business, but it gives me a glimpse into what that's like."

"*Ara* has the potential for growth. You've got some great designs, and although I don't know what system you've built around the business, I've seen your website, and I see a lot of potential. I'm proud of you, Mabel."

Mabel looked at him and was at a loss for words. Barry had never said those words to her before. Barry took advantage of her silence and covered the distance between them, his eyes not leaving hers.

"I'm going to Dubai the day after tomorrow. Come with me—just the two of us. When we get back, we can take the girls to Disney."

Mabel drank some more because a part of her wanted to say yes. She wanted to be with Barry again, to have him kiss her and make love for hours. Her body yearned for now, but her head warned her to take it slow.

"No. I only agreed to come to Disney because of the girls. But I won't come to Dubai or spend the night with you."

Barry nodded. He studied her and took a step closer. Mabel could see the unbridled desire deep in his eyes.

"What will it take?" he asked. "What do I have to do?"

She didn't know what to say. He was close, and once again, his arm went around her waist, and she was up against his chest. She should have resisted and moved out of his grasp, but she didn't and couldn't.

One little kiss wouldn't hurt, she reckoned. So, as his head lowered, she reached up, and as his lips met hers, she parted her lips slightly, inviting him in.

CHAPTER FIFTEEN

Elizabeth tucked her phone into her handbag, her heart heavy as she wiped away a tear that dared to escape.

"Mummy, are you okay?" Andrew gazed up at her, his blue eyes shimmering with a mix of worry and earnestness.

Feeling a wave of warmth from his genuine concern for her well-being, Elizabeth tilted her head slightly, a smile playing at the corners of her lips as their eyes met. Her little man was blossoming into a truly compassionate soul. He was unwell after their five-day, five-night trip to Tenerife, but he still recognised her distress.

"I'm fine, Andy," she assured him. "How about you?"

"A little better than yesterday," he replied. "Who was that on the phone? You sounded upset."

"Andrew, you're not helping by asking Mum questions. Leave her alone!" James snapped. He was in one of his surly teenage moods.

Seated in the rear of the cab between Elizabeth and James on the ride home from the airport, Andrew glanced from one to the other before bowing his head in sorrow. Elizabeth took his small hand and squeezed it as she looked out the cab window and reflected on the news she had just heard. A lot had happened in the few days she'd been out of the country on holiday.

The instant her plane touched down in London, a call had come through from Simone, a secretary at the firm, informing her of Anita's arrest earlier that day. Desmond Bailey, Anita's deadbeat partner, who fathered her children, had allegedly murdered someone in his apartment in Kent four nights ago and driven to London in the middle of the night to ask Anita, a criminal defence solicitor, how he could get rid of the evidence.

Anita had told him how to get rid of the body, but unfortunately, the body had been discovered, the deadbeat man had fled the country, and Anita had been arrested. Elizabeth knew if her dear friend was spared jail, she could be struck off, bringing her career as a solicitor to an end. But it was more likely that she was going to prison for perverting the course of justice.

As they arrived home, she went to her bedroom, asking James to prepare a light dinner for himself and his brother. Overwhelmed by her emotions, she felt utterly at a loss. All she wanted was to collapse onto her bed and let the tears flow freely, pouring out all her heartache.

"Oh, Anita. How could you do it? You didn't think of your poor children!" She sobbed as she thought of Sophie and Matthew and what would become of the young children if their mother went to prison.

Feeling the need for a shoulder to cry on, she reached for her phone on the bedside table and dialled Barry's number. A wave of relief flooded her as the phone began to ring, but that sense of hope quickly turned into disappointment when the call was abruptly rejected. She stared at her phone in disbelief that Barry had rejected her call. She tried again, disappointed when the call went straight to his voicemail. Perhaps, she had picked a particularly inopportune moment to call. After all, he could very well have been caught up in a meeting. But she needed him. Her world was falling apart.

She thought about calling John but caught herself just in time and decided against it. John was a goody-two-shoes and would likely criticise Anita for being foolish instead of offering the comfort she so desperately needed. Feeling sorry for herself because she had no one to turn to, she buried her head in her pillow again and wept softly. A movement in her room caused her to look up, and Andrew was standing just a few feet from the bed, holding his stomach.

"Are you okay, Andy?"

Without saying a word, he threw up all over the soft, shaggy rug. Elizabeth stared at the mess on her white bedside rug and cried even harder.

On the bedside table, her phone began to ring, and she eagerly reached for it, thinking it was Barry returning her call. But it was Chris calling to check in and find out how their trip went. Elizabeth answered the phone and said, "I need you to come over."

"Are you okay?" Chris was taken aback by her request.

"Do I sound like I'm okay?" Elizabeth asked in between tears.

"I'm on my way," Chris said, and Elizabeth ended the call, laying her head on the pillow, her eyelids heavy with sleep.

About fifteen minutes later, Chris arrived at the house. He rang the doorbell, and when there was no answer, he used his key and let himself into the house, shutting the door behind him and racing up the stairs. Elizabeth was lying across her bed, curled up in the foetal position and still dressed in outside clothes. He raised a brow. Elizabeth never lay on her bed wearing her outside clothes. As he approached, he looked down and saw the nasty pool of vomit.

"Andrew threw up on the rug," Elizabeth said weakly, acknowledging his presence for the first time.

"So I see. Is he okay?"

"I don't know. He came in and threw up and went back to his room." Elizabeth began to cry.

"I'll check on him and come back to clean up this mess." Chris didn't wait for an answer as he turned around and went to check on Andrew.

James was in his room playing a video game, and as Chris peered inside through the half-open door, he paused the game and took off his headset.

"Hey, Dad."

"Hey, buddy. Are you okay?"

James nodded. "What are you doing here?"

"Mum needed my help. Andrew is unwell and has been sick over her bedroom rug."

James rolled his eyes. "That would be a lot for her to handle."

"Yes, it would be, especially when you sit in your room and can't be bothered with anything going on in the house where you live."

"Sorry, Dad," James mumbled.

Chris sighed, shaking his head. "You need to be more responsible, James," he chided. "I'll talk to you later; I need to see how Andrew is doing."

Okay, Dad." James put his headset back on and once again got sucked into the game.

Chris entered Andrew's room, where the little boy was sprawled across his bed and fast asleep. He tried to help him under the covers but noticed his pyjamas were stained with vomit. So he fetched a clean pair from the chest of drawers. As he helped him get changed, Andrew woke up and smiled, framing his father's face with his small hands.

"Daddy."

"Hey, buddy. How are you feeling?"

"Andrew was sick right after dinner and couldn't sleep. And Andrew threw up."

Chris gave him a smile. "I know. I saw your vomit all over Mummy's rug."

"I didn't mean to make a mess, Daddy. I went to tell Mummy my tummy hurt, and my dinner just came out."

"But do you feel better now?"

"Yes, Daddy. But a little cold."

"Just cold?" He took Andrew's little hands in his and rubbed them. "No headache?"

Andrew shook his head. "Just cold, Daddy. No headache."

"Good. You need to go under the duvet; I'm sure you'll feel nice and warm."

"Okay, Daddy."

Once Chris had dressed Andrew in his clean pyjamas, he helped him get under the duvet and tucked it around him.

"Is that nice and warm?" he asked.

Andrew smiled. "Yes, Daddy. Thank you."

"You're welcome, son." Chris kissed his forehead and walked out of the room, turning off the light as he did.

He returned to Elizabeth's room to find her still lying across the bed in her outside clothes. She appeared to have drifted off to sleep, so he let her be as he tackled the mess on the rug until it was spick and span once again. Then he gently reached for Elizabeth, pulling her into a sitting position so he could take her clothes off. Getting Elizabeth ready for bed was something he had done countless times, but this was different. They were living apart, and he didn't know how she would react to him trying to get her out of her clothes.

But Elizabeth was quiet as he got her out of her clothes and into her pyjamas and helped her to the bathroom to remove her makeup and clean her teeth. Eventually, he helped her into bed, and as he put the duvet around her and straightened to leave, she reached out and grabbed his hand.

"Thank you, Chris. You're such a good man."

Chris was at a loss for words for a moment. Elizabeth called him a good man. What had prompted that? It couldn't be because he had come over and done tasks that he had been doing for years while they lived together, could it? She never appreciated those things then, and she certainly never said he was a good man. Which was okay because he didn't consider himself a good man, and he was certain she wouldn't if she knew him more.

"You're welcome," he said eventually. "I will check on Andrew in the morning. He appears fine. He did have a bellyache but was better after he threw up.

"All over my rug," Elizabeth added.

"He said it just came out." Chris chuckled. "He should sleep well through the night. I'll check on him in the morning, and if he needs to go to the GP, I'll take him."

"Thank you," Elizabeth said, and as he turned to leave, she added, "Please don't leave."

Stunned, Chris turned to look at her. "Is everything okay?"

"No. Anita's been arrested." Elizabeth began to cry.

Chris kicked off his shoes and climbed into bed, pulling her into his arms as he had done multiple times in the past. She went willingly as if it were the most natural thing in the world to do. He let her cry, stroking her hair gently. She would talk when she was ready. For now, he would offer her his shoulder to cry on.

"I am so sorry to burden you with my problems."

"Now you're being silly, Elizabeth. Anita is my friend too, and even if we're separated, you are still the mother of my boys, so your problems are mine."

Elizabeth looked up at Chris and compared him mentally to Anita's irresponsible partner, who didn't hesitate to get her into trouble. Chris would never put her in a similar situation. She muttered her thanks as he handed her the box of Kleenex on the bedside table. As she wiped her eyes and blew her nose, she shared with him Anita's predicament.

"The guy is a sorry excuse for a man," Chris said.

"You're right. And poor Anita is in so much trouble now. And those poor kids."

"That's why I said he is a sorry excuse for a man. He had no business dragging the mother of his children into such a mess. Now he's fled the country; if Anita goes to prison, those kids are left without a father or mother. No responsible man does that."

"Her family will probably watch the kids in the interim," Elizabeth said. "She may be granted bail."

"She risked too much for him. The man never loved her."

"He is a coward."

"A coward who never loved her," Chris added. "If he truly loved her, he would not have fled and left her to deal with the consequences. He would not have got her involved, to begin with."

"I always knew he was bad news," Elizabeth said.

"You and me both," Chris added.

Elizabeth sighed. "Poor Anita. She's worked so hard to get where she is. She doesn't deserve all this trouble. Chris, my heart is broken when I think of what the future holds for her."

Chris held her again as she wept, gently stroking her back until she succumbed to sleep. Gingerly, he eased away from her and climbed out of the bed. He turned to look at her and, unable to resist, leaned down and kissed her forehead before leaving the room.

As Chris left the room, turning off the light and leaving the door slightly open, Elizabeth opened her eyes. She heard his voice across the hall, softly ordering James to switch off the video game and go to bed. James grumbled but obeyed, and as Elizabeth turned in bed, a soft smile crept across her lips.

She nestled her head onto the pillow he had just occupied, savouring the faint trace of warmth and his lingering scent that enveloped her, creating a moment that felt both intimate and comforting. Her mind wandered to the last two hours he spent in the house and how he had brought back order in that short time. Chris looked after her in ways no other man did. As she drifted off to sleep, she wondered if she had made the right decision by letting him go.

***

Chris entered his car and pulled out of Elizabeth's driveway, his mind occupied with thoughts of Anita and how he was similar to her partner, Desmond. While he may not have put Elizabeth in a situation where she may go to prison, he had put her in a difficult situation, nonetheless.

She married him believing that her life would be easy, and she would have the finer things in life. He had ruined that dream by sabotaging his business. The weight of his guilt anchored him in place, preventing any chance of moving forward. He quickly judged Desmond when he wasn't too different.

As Chris crossed the threshold into his stunning two-bedroom flat, he was immediately enveloped by an aura of sophistication. The modern design, paired with luxurious furnishings, created an inviting ambience that felt both elegant and welcoming.

"What took you so long?" Ava observed him through her oversized glasses and wrinkled her nose. "I thought you'd forgotten I was waiting for you."

He smiled at the young woman who had been a great help over the past few weeks, brainstorming with him and conducting research as he planned to revive his old business. And to think he had nearly turned her down when she initially offered to help him. Ava was a responsible young lady and great at looking after James and Andrew, but that didn't mean she could be his personal assistant or carry out administrative tasks.

However, he had been mistaken. After she had persistently urged him, he finally agreed to give her a trial, and she proved to be invaluable.

They often worked in his flat when she wasn't at Elizabeth's, caring for James and Andrew. Tonight, they were developing the business plan for his new company when Elizabeth's call interrupted them. He had abandoned everything to be with his wife and kids. He knew Ava was upset; tightening her lips when he announced earlier that he was going to Elizabeth's had indicated as much.

She probably thought he indulged Elizabeth's every whim and fancy too easily, but Elizabeth was his wife, and despite their problems, he loved her. Until they divorced, she was his to look after, protect, and provide for. Moreover, neither Ava nor his extended family were in any position to judge Elizabeth. They didn't know enough about him, her, or their marriage to make any judgments.

"Elizabeth wanted to talk, and there was some cleaning up to do." He dropped on the sofa and put his feet on the coffee table, crossing them at the ankles.

Ava leaned back in her chair at the dining table, the soft light of the open-plan kitchen casting a warm glow around her. She momentarily paused her typing, glancing up from her laptop and nibbling on the bottom of her pen as she considered him.

"You're a good man, Chris," she said, glancing away from him to her computer screen. "Too good to be true."

"You know the old saying: if it's too good to be true, then it likely isn't." A chuckle from Chris was followed by Ava's laughter. "I'm not a good man, Ava. I'm just a man who loves his family."

A man trying to make amends, he thought to himself.

"Hmm…" Ava chewed the bottom of her pen. "I'm sure they appreciate all you do for them."

Chris shrugged as he rose and looked at her computer screen. "Have you made any progress?"

"Not much. I wondered why you don't want to use your old business name. You could modify it a little."

Chris flinched and shook his head. It was out of the question. David-West had been ruined as far as real estate development went. He couldn't use that name again, not after how the original company ended. This was a new start; he needed something different. Ava had been thinking about a name before he went to Elizabeth's and had given him some suggestions, all of which he rejected. He could see from her screen that she'd come up with more names. He frowned because he didn't like any of them.

"David-West has long been laid to rest. This is a different company and a new beginning. I don't want to contaminate it with the negativity tied to David-West."

"You speak like it's your fault. Chris, it was an accident."

Chris met her gaze. Everyone thought it was an accident. It had been reported as an accident, but it had been no accident. But he couldn't tell her that, couldn't tell her what had really transpired. It was a secret he kept buried deep, terrified that if Elizabeth discovered the truth, she would see him as a monster. He pressed his fingers to his temple, feeling the familiar throb of an impending headache taking hold.

"Regardless, David-West is gone forever. A new beginning needs a new business name."

Ava sighed. "Okay. Do you like any of these?" She pointed to her computer screen.

Chris shook his head without hesitation. "No."

"Any suggestions?"

"Princewill."

"Princewill?" Ava looked confused.

Chris shrugged. "It was my mother's maiden name. I have used my surname, so maybe it's time to try my mother's."

"Ah. I see." Ava turned to her computer screen and typed the business name on the front cover of the plan. "Princewill it is. Now, let's hope your investors like it."

Chris looked at his wristwatch. It was almost time for his first meeting with two old business partners. They were the only two who had remained connected with him after his world had crashed. He hoped they would buy into his new vision, but worried they would be sceptical after the incident with David-West Tower.

Ava thought he didn't need investors and could start small using his money. But Elizabeth wanted something different, and this was all about her and the boys, trying to prove to her that he had what it took to keep her in the style she was accustomed to. He wanted to show the boys that when a man fell, he had to try to get back on his feet. So, while he could start small, it would take a long time to grow that way, and he was better off succeeding, starting with other people's money.

"I'm sure they'll be more interested in how I intend to make them good money," Chris pointed out. "We have an hour before the meeting. Is it okay if I sleep for a bit?"

Ava nodded. "Sure. Lie down. I'll wake you when it's time."

"You're a divine blessing, Ava." Chris beamed at her. "My life is so much better because of you.

"You could consider giving me a tremendous bonus at the end of the summer when my contract ends."

Chris laughed. "I'll think about it."

Inside his bedroom, he kicked off his shoes and lay on the bed. As soon as he closed his eyes, visions of David-West, the fallen Tower, and the mounting death toll of the subsequent days plagued him. His dear friend Alabo had died, leaving behind a wife and two daughters. He pictured their final moments together, which was interrupted by the call from James's nanny. She sounded frantic.

"Sir, come right away," she told him. "James is vomiting his lunch. I think he is ill."

"Alabo, I need to see my son. I will be back soon," he told his friend, a much older man he employed as a site foreman on the David-West Tower project.

Alabo gave him a thumbs up, as he descended to the ground floor using the improvised elevator built for workers to transport materials between floors. His Land Cruiser and driver awaited him on the grounds. He climbed in and shut the door, removing his hard hat, and cleaning the dust from his suit.

"Take me to the house," he instructed.

On the short drive to his waterfront mansion, he called his doctor. James was being examined when a commotion erupted outside among the domestic staff. Before he could bolt out to find out what was happening, his driver hurried through the front door, urgency etched across his face.

"Sir, come out quick and look. David-West Tower has collapsed!"

He rushed out to the balcony, where he could always see the unfinished high-rise residential building in the distance. However, at that moment, a thick cloud of dust swirling through the air obscured his vision, shrouding everything in a gritty haze. All around him, chaos broke out on the streets as anguished cries and heart-wrenching wails pierced the air, echoing outside his gate. A sudden, searing pain pierced through his left side, forcing him to stumble. As the world around him blurred, he could feel gravity pulling him down, the ground rushing up to meet him.

With a sudden jolt, he shot upright in bed, his heart racing. "No!" he cried out as the remnants of his dream faded into the shadows of the night.

"Chris!" Ava rushed into the room and sat on the edge of the bed. "Are you okay?"

He nodded. Not knowing if he could trust himself to speak. He buried his head in his hands. Was he ready for this? Was he ready to try again? After the deaths? He thought of his good friend, Alabo, who died because of him. He saw the bodies that were removed from the site. Not just workers. There were women who sold food to the workers. They were breadwinners of their families and had perished, leaving behind children who would be desolate. All because of him.

He flinched as Ava's arm touched his shoulder in a comforting gesture. She wouldn't be helping him rebuild his business if she knew what kind of man he was. Young and naïve, she saw his sacrifice for an indifferent wife and idolised him. She thought him a saint, but Chris David-West was no saint.

CHAPTER SIXTEEN

Mabel had been in her house!

Victoria knew it. She sensed it, but she couldn't explain how. So, a few days after their return, she looked at the CCTV, which had picked up Mabel. She asked John, who said Mabel had brought him a home-cooked meal as the family had been away. The evening before they were due back. How generous of her, Victoria had sneered without meaning to. She had expected John to rebuke her as usual when she acted unlovingly towards anyone. To her surprise, he hadn't. What was more, he looked very guilty and quickly changed the subject.

His behaviour was out of character and had got her thinking. What did John have to be guilty about regarding Mabel's visit to the house? Was there more? Something he wasn't telling her? And why did Mabel choose to visit her home in her absence? And then there was the car. She had taken delivery of a brand-new Mercedes Benz today. It was a surprise as she had not expected John to change her car. John wouldn't buy her a new car unless he wished to appease her. Appease her for what? Had he slept with Mabel? Had she tried to seduce him, and he had fallen? Was that it?

Well, whatever it was, it didn't matter. Victoria was done playing the role of the quiet, dutiful wife who saw everything but said nothing. She was different. Something had changed inside of her when John failed to make the trip to Texas. She had looked forward to the trip, to having her husband to herself for an entire week and rekindling the marriage and what little romance had once been in it.

When he gave her the lingerie, she'd been hopeful that, like her, he also wanted to rekindle the spark in their marriage. But when he had cancelled the trip for something as small as Mabel's child being ill, she'd known she couldn't go on. She had spent the time away thinking deeply about her marriage and had reached the conclusion that she was better off without John. He didn't need a wife. She was tired of being ignored until the moment when he wanted sex. No more of that. She wanted to be with a man who loved her and would choose her and prioritise her above everything else. John could never be that man. She realised it many years and three children too late.

She returned from holiday to inform John that she was leaving him and planned to relocate to Texas with the kids. In Texas, she would be close to her sister and mother, who would support her in rebuilding her life. She would find work and finally be able to use her biomedical science degree. The kids would be fine. She hadn't discussed her plans but knew they would be okay. The status quo wasn't really going to change; it wasn't as if they saw their father now.

Lost in thought about the future, Victoria looked up just as Lindsay stepped into the living room, gracefully ushering Pastor Alan inside. The atmosphere shifted as Victoria prepared to welcome her guest.

Pastor Alan was a soft-spoken white British man in his late sixties, not prone to using too many words. He was a travelling minister with a small church congregation in Primrose Hill. Alan had known John since he was a boy living in South Africa and had mentored him for over thirty years.

Victoria invited him for a conversation because she had great respect and admiration for him. He married her and John in his church, and she thought she owed it to him to tell him that she was leaving John. She didn't care what anyone else thought about her decision, but she cared about what Alan thought, so she invited him.

She stood up, smiling, glad to see him and appreciative that he could take time from his busy schedule to visit her at her request.

"Hello, Victoria. How are you? You look well," Alan greeted as he moved closer and embraced Victoria.

"Thank you, Alan." With a smile, Victoria withdrew from the embrace. "You look very well yourself. Thank you for coming to see me at such short notice."

"Anything for an old friend, Victoria." Pastor Alan patted Victoria's arm gently. "You and John are very dear friends to me, and whatever I can do to help, I am more than happy to do."

Victoria knew this was true; Alan had been a faithful friend to herself and John even before they were married and had always been there for them when they needed him. Victoria had never mentioned to him the challenges in her marriage to John because she had never seen the need to. So what she was about to tell him would come as quite a surprise, especially as she had reached the decision to end the marriage.

In retrospect, Victoria couldn't help but wonder if she had done the right thing in not bringing her marital issues to Alan's attention before now. Perhaps an older man whom John respected and who, like him, was also a pastor could have helped John see his errors.

"Thank you, Alan." She waved to the sofa. "Please sit down. Can I get you anything to drink? Tea, coffee, perhaps?"

Alan shook his head. "Nothing for me, thank you, Victoria," he replied. "Let's take care of you; that's why I am here." He sat back on the sofa and patted the space next to him. "Come and tell Uncle Alan what the matter is."

Victoria laughed, suddenly feeling at ease as she sat beside him on the sofa.

"It's about John," she blurted out.

"I already suspected that," Alan said. "What about John?"

"I was hoping you would have a word with him," Victoria said, pausing. "I'm getting myself confused. It doesn't matter whether you talk to him. I've decided to leave him."

Alan raised a brow, the only indication he had heard her. She waited for him to speak, and when he didn't, she went on.

"John is becoming more and more distant from me and the kids. He's very involved in church activities and helping members, and since we've been married, it's taken up a considerable amount of his time. I assumed that at some point, it would get better, but it hasn't. It has become worse. I have tried to talk to him in the past, but he accused me of being selfish and not wanting him to help others. That isn't true; I want him to help others but not to the detriment of our family."

Alan remained in deep reflection long after Victoria finished speaking. "So you would like me to speak to John about making more time for you and the children."

"Yes, I would," Victoria affirmed. "Alan, you're a pastor and have been in the ministry longer than John has. Your experience surpasses his. You can counsel him. Or am I being unreasonable?"

"Not as far as I can see, no." He gazed intently at her. "Is this all you wanted to discuss with me, or is there something else?"

"That's it, really. And although I ask you to speak to him, I'm done, Alan. Living like this is no longer acceptable. I plan to take the kids and move to America."

Alan exhaled. "Victoria, you can't ask me to speak with John when your mind's already made up."

Victoria nodded in agreement. "I should have said something earlier, but I didn't want to be perceived as a terrible wife betraying her husband by taking our marital problems to a third party."

Alan patted her knee gently. "I can understand that. But now that you've brought the matter to me, can you put away any thoughts of ending this marriage from your mind until I've at least had a chance to speak to John?"

"I can do that."

"Good. And I need you to understand that it may not end with me talking to John. Depending on how my conversation with him goes, you may both need to come in to see me for counselling. Are you willing to do that?"

Victoria nodded. "Yes, Alan."

"We're making progress," he stated. "Now, should counselling require changing your behaviour, are you willing to do that?"

Victoria's eyes widened in disbelief as she gazed at him, her mind racing to comprehend the absurdity of his words. "Oh, Alan, I'm sure you'll find that the issue is entirely with John and not me."

"Victoria?" Alan prompted gently.

Victoria sighed. "Yes, Alan, I will be willing to make changes on my part."

"Excellent!" Alan applauded. "Leave it with me. I'll speak with John, and we'll take it from there. Don't pack your bags yet."

Victoria nodded in agreement. She respected and admired Alan and was willing to do as he instructed.

***

"I noticed that both of you arrived for church separately on Sunday, and I instantly sensed a problem. Would you mind telling me what's going on?"

John leaned back in his chair and looked from Pastor Maranatha Obasi to his wife, Beatrice. They were a young interracial couple: Pastor Maranatha hailed from the vibrant Igbo tribe in Enugu, Africa, and his wife Beatrice was a white British woman. The couple were long-standing church members and married in The Vine Church five years ago. John officiated at their wedding and, a year after, employed Pastor Maranatha as the church's youth pastor.

"What's going on?" John asked again as no response was forthcoming.

Beatrice looked at Maranatha and then at John. "He moved out."

"Only because you asked me to!" Maranatha snapped.

John sat up and held up both hands. "Calm down, you two. I have called this meeting to understand the situation. Pastor Maranatha, you don't need me to tell you that in your role as a youth pastor, you are a role model not only to the youth in The Vine Church but also to thousands of young people across this country who follow the church's youth programmes."

Beatrice looked away, and Pastor Maranatha sighed and bowed his head. "I understand this, Pastor John."

"Good," John said. "Why did you leave home? You've said Beatrice asked you to leave. But why? What's the problem?"

"We had a fight." It was Beatrice who replied.

"A fight about what exactly?" John looked from husband to wife.

"We've been trying for a baby for four years. It's important to me that he's around during my ovulation but he has other commitments that mean he is often away. Three months ago, I started taking fertility boost supplements. I was asked to take it for three months before trying. Maranatha knew this. Once I completed the supplements, his sister called from Enugu, and he hopped on a plane and was gone for four days. When he returned, we argued. I said he had put his family before ours. He said I was being unreasonable because I would have other ovulations."

"And you asked him to leave the house?"

"Not at first. But then he said we'd been trying for four years, and he didn't see why I had to get so hung up on the fact that he was away for four days. He said, Beatrice, if you were going to get pregnant, four years is more than enough time." Beatrice sobbed. "He also said I was lucky he was a Christian, and it was the only reason he had not succumbed to his family's pressure for him to take a wife from Enugu who would bear him children."

While Beatrice wept quietly, John's gaze fell on Pastor Maranatha, who avoided his eyes.

"Did you say that to your wife, Pastor Maranatha?" he asked.

Pastor Maranatha met his gaze briefly. "Yes. I did. But I didn't mean it. I was feeling frustrated."

"So, what do you want to do now?"

"I am happy to do whatever Beatrice wants." Pastor Maranatha passed his sobbing wife a handkerchief.

John looked at Beatrice. "Beatrice, what do you want? I am going to join my faith with yours now and pray for you. But I need to know what your heart desires in line with God's word."

Beatrice wiped her eyes and looked up at John. "I want to have children."

"Is that what you want, Pastor Maranatha?"

Pastor Maranatha nodded. "Yes, Pastor John."

John rose and picked up the bottle of anointing oil on his desk. Instantly, both Pastor Maranatha and Beatrice pushed back their chairs and knelt down.

"I want both of you to ask each other and God for forgiveness. David said in the Scriptures, if I regard iniquity in my heart, the Lord will not hear me."

As he walked round his desk to stand before the couple, he observed them shyly offering apologies to one another. He shut his eyes and worshipped for a minute before the Lord, giving them time to make amends before the Lord.

He anointed each on the forehead. "In nine months, return with your child or children. Have the children as you want them, male or female, single or multiple births. The delay is over in the name of Jesus. Amen."

Pastor Maranatha stood to his feet and helped Beatrice up, pulling her close and kissing her cheek. John smiled and returned to stand by his chair, putting down the bottle of oil before looking up at the couple.

"You need to return home immediately, Pastor Maranatha. We have prayed. God has answered. But it will not be an immaculate conception."

The couple laughed and thanked him and made their way out of his office. As they left, Liam peered into the room.

"Pastor Alan is here to see you," he announced.

John frowned. He didn't remember arranging to meet with Alan. "Send him in." He shoved his hands deep into his pockets as he waited for Liam to show Alan in.

Alan stepped into the room, and Liam shut the door behind him. He smiled at John as he approached the desk.

"How are you, John?" he asked as they shook hands.

"I am very well, thank you, Alan. And yourself? Please have a sit."

"I am well, John. The Lord has been faithful." Alan sank into one of the chairs on the other side of the desk as John took his place behind his desk.

"And Harriet?" John asked.

"She's doing well," Alan said. "I haven't seen you in a while."

John sat back in his chair, crossing his legs at the ankles. "You know what pastoring a church is like, Alan."

Pastor Alan nodded. "Indeed, I do," he said. "And speaking of the church, how are things at The Vine Church?"

"Things are fine at The Vine Church. I apologise for not keeping in contact more frequently; it has been a bit busy for me lately."

"So I hear," Alan said. "I was with Victoria earlier today."

Both men locked eyes. John realised at that moment why Alan had visited him. His eyes narrowed, and his teeth clenched as he struggled to control his temper. This better not be what he thought it was. Victoria had better keep their marital issues private and off the table for everyone else to see. He had a policy that required them to resolve their issues without involving a third party, and Victoria had adhered to it thus far. She'd been withdrawn since returning from holiday, even in bed. Not that she denied him sex, but he could tell her heart wasn't in it. He thought getting her new car would change that, but when the car arrived this morning, she had not been as thrilled as he'd expected.

"You know, John, it's okay if you can't make time for your old mentor, but it's not okay if you can't make time for your own family."

John tensed. "Did Victoria tell you that I spend no time with my family?" he asked.

"Yes," Alan replied after a long silence. "She's only concerned, John. And she has a right to be. She's your wife."

John lifted both hands and ran them through his hair.

"Sometimes, I don't understand the woman I married. She knew when she was marrying me that God had called me to be a pastor, and she was aware that it was a task that would demand my time. Why does she continue to make a fuss about it? Alan, I'm busy. My job is demanding, but once every year, I take Victoria and the kids away on holiday so we can be together as a family. We didn't go last summer, and I couldn't travel with them this summer, but that isn't enough for Victoria to act as if I've failed in my duties as a husband and father."

Alan paused thoughtfully, considering John's words. "A holiday once a year is good, John, but it takes more than a few weeks holiday every year to be a good husband and father. Make more time for your family, John. Your success as a pastor lies largely on your success as a husband and father. The Bible admonishes the man who desires to be a bishop. A man that cannot look after his family cannot look after God's church."

John did not respond; he remained silent, seething in anger.

CHAPTER SEVENTEEN

Elizabeth looked away from the computer screen and rubbed her eyes as her phone rang. A warm smile spread across her face the moment she recognised Barry's name, lighting up her screen. She had been caught off guard by his call, especially since it had been over a week since she had last heard from him. He had deliberately ignored her calls, leaving them unanswered and her messages hanging in silence.

She assumed he was just caught up in his own world. Yet, deep down, a nagging worry began to creep in—what if he was slowly slipping away from her? They had not recently gone on any trips together, and Barry always travelled. So, he either went alone or took someone else with him. She found it too uncomfortable to even entertain the thought of the latter.

"Hello, darling," she cooed, her voice a sultry whisper as she playfully tossed her hair over her shoulder. Leaning back in her chair, she smiled captivatingly, promising secrets yet to unfold. "This is a pleasant surprise. Were you missing me?"

Barry drew in his breath sharply as he drummed his fingers on his steering wheel. He had not missed

Elizabeth. The only time he had thought of her in the last fortnight was as he plotted to end their affair so he could get together with Mabel. He had lost every desire for her. Not even when Mabel refused to go with him to Dubai had he considered inviting Elizabeth.

And he was glad he hadn't. He was also happy he hadn't been with any woman during the Dubai trip because as soon as he returned, he took Mabel and the girls to Paris. He wouldn't have been able to enjoy the trip or the time in Mabel's presence if he'd been guilt-ridden about sleeping with another woman only days before.

"We need to talk. I learnt you were working from home today, so I thought I'd come to your house. I am sitting in my car in front of your house. Let me in."

Elizabeth's eyes widened in disbelief, a wave of surprise washing over her as she tried to comprehend what he'd just said. Barry had never been to her home because it would have been awkward while Chris lived there. Even after Chris moved out, Barry never seemed interested and preferred for her to come to his place instead.

"Are you serious? You're sitting in your car outside my house? Well, come on in then."

She ended the call, tossed her mobile phone onto a pile of papers on her desk and hurried to the front door. Barry had chosen the perfect time to visit as she was home alone. The boys were with Chris, who had been taking them on daily sightseeing trips in London and Kent since the beginning of that week.

They would have a bit of time to themselves before the boys returned. Excitedly, she opened the door to find

Barry, who looked handsome in a blue three-piece Italian business suit. She pulled him inside by the lapels of his jacket and slammed the door shut behind him. As her lips brushed his, he grasped her hands and gently held her away.

"We need to talk, Elizabeth."

Surprised by his unexpected behaviour, Elizabeth raised an eyebrow and shrugged, trying to mask her bewilderment. "Sure. This way."

She guided him into the living room and took a seat, crossing her legs to reveal her thighs. She beamed warmly, her eyes sparkling with invitation as she motioned to the empty space beside her on the sofa, a welcoming gesture that felt impossible to resist.

"Sit down," she said.

Barry ignored the gesture and took the chair opposite her.

"I'm ending our relationship." He wasted no time diving into the purpose of his visit, meeting her gaze with intensity as his words flowed.

Elizabeth's breath caught in her throat, her eyes widening in disbelief. She had never anticipated such a twist so quickly. Lately, he had been acting strangely, not taking her calls or responding to her texts, but she assumed he was under pressure from work. Yes, she feared there might be another woman, someone younger and more beautiful, but she thought it was a phase they would overcome.

"Why?" she asked. "Is it another woman?"

Barry's gaze was unwavering as it held hers, creating an electric connection that seemed to pause time around them. "It is another woman, but it's also Jesus. Mainly Jesus."

He'd made a heartfelt promise to Jesus that if Daisy's health was restored, he would return to his family without hesitation. Daisy was healed, so it was time to fulfil the promise. He could not get back together with Mabel and carry on with Elizabeth. He was not that man anymore.

As soon as Jesus' name was mentioned, Elizabeth couldn't hold back any longer; a burst of dry, mirthless laughter erupted from her, filling the room. "That's the most ridiculous thing I ever heard. Jesus? Are you being serious?"

He nodded. "Yes, Elizabeth. I'm serious. I met Jesus and fell in love with my wife again. And I need to pursue a relationship with both Jesus and my wife; I can't do that with you on the side. I'm sorry." He rose to his feet and thrust his hands into his trouser pockets.

Elizabeth shot up from her seat, her eyes blazing with intensity as she folded her arms defiantly across her chest. "So, you met Jesus, did you? Well, I have always known Jesus. He was in my house all the years of my childhood and adulthood. My father was a missionary, made poor by Jesus, and my brother is a preacher, called away from a lucrative career to a thankless job by Jesus, so don't come here and speak to me as if you know something I don't."

"I don't know if we are talking about the same Jesus, Elizabeth. I only know that Jesus answered my heartfelt prayer, and I want to walk with Him for the rest of my life."

"Fine then. But let me warn you. I have known Jesus longer than you have. He lets people down. And don't come running to me when He lets you down, as I am sure He soon will."

Barry strolled towards the front door and paused to glance at Elizabeth. "I'm certain now that we're not referring to the same person, Elizabeth. Goodbye."

As he turned toward the door, Elizabeth let out a gasp. "I don't believe this! You're just going to walk away like that?" she demanded. "I sent my husband away because of you!"

He abruptly halted, and he pivoted to meet her gaze, irritation sparking in his eyes. "You told me when we met that the marriage had long ceased to exist, and you led separate lives, although living under the same roof."

He waited for her to refute the statement, and when she didn't, he shrugged. "Don't make me responsible for your problems, Elizabeth." He opened the door and walked out, shutting it firmly behind him.

Elizabeth picked a cushion and tossed it at the door. It hit the front door and fell to the floor.

"I hope you rot in hell, Barry Babs-Jonah!" she cried.

She marched towards the front door and picked up the cushion, tossing it carelessly into the living room as she returned to her home office. The man's nerve! He wanted a relationship with Jesus and his ex-wife—and after she had let her husband go! Barry had been a huge mistake.

She saw that now. He never cared for her. And while being with him had made her more prosperous and advanced her career, he had not treated her with the same kindness and gentleness that Chris had. In and out of bed, it had been clear that her body was all he desired. He had not been interested in her as a person. She couldn't remember one time he had wanted to discuss her life. He centred their conversations on her work only when it related to his, and when not discussing her work, he focused on travel plans because he wanted sex.

Chris had been interested in her from the beginning, wanting to know her dreams and how he could help her accomplish them. He cared deeply about her well-being and would do anything to ensure she and the boys were all right. Even after asking him to leave the house, he still showed up for her when she wanted him to.

What had she done? She buried her head in her hands and groaned.

Why did she let go of a man who loved her to pursue someone who did not care about her? What was she seeking? Money? Chris had money once. And Chris could make money again. If she'd been patient and encouraged him, his desire to care for her would have driven him to strive for more. But instead of being patient, she nagged. Instead of affirming him, she made him feel less of a man. But hopefully, it wasn't too late. They had only been separated for a few months. Surely, she could still get him back.

Suddenly, the door swung open, and the boys dashed into the hall, slamming it shut behind them. The sound of their laughter filled the foyer, bubbling up and spilling throughout the entire house like a joyful melody.

"Serves you right!" Andrew shrieked, and James roared with laughter.

"Keep the noise down, you two; I'm trying to get some work done." Elizabeth raced out of her study.

"Sorry, Mum," James and Andrew mumbled.

With her hands firmly planted on her hips, she gazed at them intently, her expression filled with revulsion. "You both look filthy. I don't know what you've been up to, but please go upstairs and shower."

"Okay, Mum." James took Andrew by the hand and together they walked past her towards the stairs.

Elizabeth's nose crinkled in distaste as she watched them depart. "Have you had dinner?"

"Yes. We went to MacDonalds on the way home," Andrew said.

"Where's Dad?" she asked, wondering why Chris had not come to the door with the boys as he usually did when he brought them home.

"Dad's dropping Ava off. He should be on the other side of the road," James said as he led Andrew up the stairs.

Elizabeth stood frozen, her brow furrowing in confusion. Chris was dropping off Ava? The unexpected turn of events left her mind racing. What could it possibly mean?

"Why is Dad dropping Ava off? Did you pick her up on the way here?"

"Ava came with us!" Andrew said excitedly.

"Yes. Dad invited her," James confirmed.

With a burst of energy, Elizabeth dashed into the living room and yanked the heavy curtains aside. Her heart raced as she pressed her face to the glass, eager to glimpse the world outside. The boys were right. Chris's car was parked in front of Ava's house, across the road, and as the day wasn't yet dark, a glimpse of him and Ava in a car, laughing and leaning close together in deep conversation, caught her eye. After a few minutes, Ava exited the car and teasingly blew Chris a kiss as he drove off.

"Oh, this is too much!" Elizabeth muttered as she dashed into the hallway, looking around for her car keys. "James, watch your brother for a minute. I'll be back soon!"

"Mum, where're you going?" Andrew raced to the top of the stairs, and James chased after him to stop him.

"I'm going to Dad's. I won't be long."

With a dramatic flair, she snatched her keys and left the house, slamming the door shut. She would only be gone for a few minutes. The boys would be fine. She had to give that lying, cheating husband of hers a piece of her mind.

His flat was about five minutes' drive away. Her heart raced as she sped down the street, and with a surge of frustration, she hammered on his front door, each knock echoing her mounting anger.

"Elizabeth, is everything okay?" Chris looked surprised to see her as he opened his front door and let her into his apartment.

"How long have you been seeing Ava?" Elizabeth turned to face him in the narrow, wood-panelled hallway.

Chris raised a brow in surprise. "Seeing Ava? You mean as in dating her?"

"You know what I mean, Christopher Chimbiko David-West! I saw you both in your car earlier. Talking and laughing. You and the young woman I hire to watch the kids. How long have you been cheating on me with her?"

"Elizabeth, if you're looking for grounds for divorce, this won't fly. I've never cheated on you with Ava. Ava is a friend and nothing more. She's great with the kids, and has been useful in helping me furnish this place and set up my business."

Elizabeth was stunned. Ava had helped Chris furnish his apartment and set up his business. What business? She knew nothing about any business.

"You're setting up a new business?"

"I thought it was time to return to work as a real estate developer. I set up a new company, Princewill Consortium, and Ava has helped with the admin side. She's been a great one-man army, and we've achieved a lot together since she's been on summer vacation from university. But I'm not sleeping with her. I've never slept with her."

Elizabeth looked at the man she had married and tried to see him from another woman's eyes for the first time. Handsome, well-built, intelligent, and caring, only a stupid woman would pass up the opportunity to capture him. Ava might be his friend. Perhaps he hadn't slept with her, but for how long?

If she furnished his apartment, was involved in his business, and went on outings with him and the boys, it was only a matter of time before he slept with her. She had not had sex with him for months before she threw him out. Ava was a smart young woman and wouldn't waste time seducing him. In Ava's shoes, she would. She noticed that while he said he'd never slept with Ava, he had not said he didn't want to.

"I didn't know about this. About your business or involvement with Ava."

"It's still early days with the business, and there hasn't been time to tell you about it. Besides, I didn't think you'd be interested. As for Ava, it's strictly platonic. She gets a small fee for her work for me, and that's it."

"But you spend a lot of time together."

"Yes! Because we're working together!" Chris was becoming a little frustrated. He had never seen Ava as a potential lover.

Elizabeth nodded, unsure of what to say next and feeling foolish. "I must be going. Please accept my apologies for wrongly accusing you. It surprised me you and Ava were involved—I never considered it."

"We're not involved," Chris corrected. "You're misinterpreting the situation. She's my friend, Elizabeth. I'm incredibly grateful for her help in getting back on my feet, but she's not romantically involved with me; and speaking of Ava, who's looking after the boys?"

"James is watching Andrew. I told them I'd return shortly."

Chris shook his head with a sigh. "Then you should be on your way."

She nodded, but she couldn't bring herself to leave. How could she have overlooked Ava and Chris spending time together? Given Ava's daily support in rebuilding his business, how long before he falls in love with her and commits? If that occurred, would he continue supporting her and the boys? If he didn't, who would?

John was in high demand, so he couldn't be there for her every time she called for him. Barry had shown her that just because a man found her attractive and wanted her body didn't mean she could count on him. So far, Chris was her only support, but due to her own mistakes, she was on the verge of losing him to a younger, more attractive woman.

What had driven her to reject him was no longer relevant. Barry was gone, and Chris worked to rebuild his business. Soon, he would regain his high-powered business life, but would his feelings for her remain? And if Chris rejected her, who would look after her?

A sob escaped her lips without warning. Chris was perplexed.

"Elizabeth. What's wrong?" he asked.

Silent tears streamed down her cheeks as she struggled to find her voice. He let out a deep sigh, his heart aching for her pain, and drew her into his embrace, holding her close as she surrendered to the moment.

CHAPTER EIGHTEEN

"Victoria!" John called as he stepped into the house, walking briskly to his home office and dropping his briefcase on the desk. He took off his suit jacket and tossed it onto the armchair by his desk. He then yanked at his tie and unbuttoned the top button of his shirt, which suddenly made his throat feel constricted.

As Victoria moved around the kitchen, guiding Lindsay in preparing meals for the following day, she suddenly froze, startled by John's voice echoing through the air as he called her name. He sounded very angry, and she wondered whether Alan had spoken to him already. Smiling apologetically at Lindsay, she left the kitchen and followed the direction of his voice. The office door was open, and John stood in the middle of the room, rolling up his shirt sleeves.

"What's the matter?" she inquired, stepping into the room and positioning herself gracefully beside the open doorway.

John paused and looked up at her. "You took our affairs to Alan." It was not a question but a statement.

Victoria took a deep breath, her throat tightening as she brushed a strand of hair behind her ear, a nervous habit that revealed her anticipation. Perhaps she had made a mistake. John hated to have third parties involved in their affairs. She should have just told him she wanted a divorce and not dragged Alan in.

"Yes, I did." She braced herself for what would follow.

John threw his hands up in the air. "I don't believe this. So now you take issues in our marriage out and try to make people think that I neglect you and that I am a bad husband? What haven't I done for you, Victoria?" he asked. As she remained silent, he went on. "You live in a beautiful house, bought in your name. You have never worked a day since we were married. I pay you a generous salary, which is possibly more than women who work earn. You drive a luxurious car and...."

"That's not enough to make you a good husband, Dad." John Jr. entered the office, stepping in between John and Victoria.

John looked at him in utter astonishment and then turned to Victoria. "You've trained the kids to speak back to me, Victoria?"

Victoria was on the brink of tears and couldn't bring herself to respond. How could she have loved this man who didn't love her? She had spoken to Alan, hoping he could persuade John to listen because she never seemed able to get him to. But Alan had failed, and this marked the end of her marriage.

Her heart was breaking, and tears streamed down her face, but she was determined that after tonight, she would take her kids and move to America to begin a new life with her mother and sister. They would support her. She was done with John. He could keep his house, the luxury car, and the generous salary he paid her.

"It's not her singular responsibility to raise us, Dad; it's both your collective responsibility. Therefore, if anything isn't to your liking, don't blame her. She's done what she knows to do. You know more, but you're never around to teach it."

John could not believe his ears. "Listen to me, young man; I am your father and…"

"And it's time I told you the truth." John Jr. cut him off once again. "This family is being destroyed by your own hands. Your actions are deeply hurting your wife. You preach to men to order their priorities; I've heard you say that God ought to come first in a man's life and, after God, his family before his job. But you haven't followed that order. For you, it's God first, then your job as pastor second, then other families third and then your own family comes last. Mum has put up with it for years; I've watched her disappointment time after time as you cancelled a family outing, meal or holiday because another family needed you. If she thought having someone else speak to you would do some good, I don't think she's done anything wrong. I hope your pride will allow you to see the truth before it's too late."

John raised his hand and struck John Jr. hard across the face. Victoria's breath caught in her throat, her hands flying up to cover her mouth in shock as disbelief washed over her. It wasn't like John to hit the children. She wanted to reach out and pull John Jr. away, but he was already in one of those moods that made him resemble his father. For the next few minutes, the two men locked eyes, their gazes heavy with unspoken words and tension. John Jr. tightened his fists, a storm brewing behind his eyes, while Victoria's heart raced in response.

Don't do it, John Jr. Please, don't do it! The words echoed in her mind as panic surged within her.

"Go ahead." John leaned in, bringing their faces close together until they were eye to eye.

John Jr. was nearly as tall as he was, and they sized each other up, both ignoring Victoria, who watched from the sidelines, her hands clasped over her mouth and tears streaming down her cheeks. Suddenly, John Jr. smiled and shook his head, unclenching his fist and stepping back.

"Simply because I have the ability to do something doesn't mean that I should do it. I've spoken my mind. I'll go now." As he walked out of the study, he turned one last time to look at John, unshed tears in his eyes. "You should listen more to your messages, Pastor John."

Victoria turned and pursued him without a glance at John, wiping her tears away furiously as she walked briskly down the hall. She reached him just as he arrived at the front door.

"Are you okay?" she asked, gently touching the side of his face, which was red and bore John's fingerprints.

John Jr. jerked his head, causing her to withdraw her hand. "I'm fine, Mum, don't make a fuss." He opened the door.

"Where are you going?"

John Jr. closed the door with a soft click and squeezed his eyes shut as he inhaled deeply, filling his lungs with a sense of calm. "I need to be alone with the Lord before I sin against Him."

He opened the door and stepped out without a backward glance, and he could feel Victoria's eyes on him as he walked down the drive. He knew that he had upset her, but he really needed some time alone, or he might do something they would all regret. At the end of the driveway, he paused, contemplating which direction to take. After making his decision, he thrust his hands into his jeans pockets and began walking along the road leisurely, praying quietly as he went.

He prayed for himself and asked God's forgiveness for speaking to his father disrespectfully. He desired God's peace in his heart again and prayed until he sensed the peace return. Next, he prayed for his father and asked God to deal with the pride in his heart so he could see that he was hurting their family. Their holiday had not felt like a true vacation. His mother tried to put on a happy countenance each day, but he knew she was miserable, and her misery frustrated him.

He prayed that God would help his father to become a better husband so his mother could be a happier woman. In praying for his father, he also prayed for his mother, asking God to comfort her and heal her broken heart. Finally, he prayed for his siblings. Rebekah and Paul engaged in foolishness that his father may never be aware of until it became a significant issue and a major embarrassment. Just like his mother longed for her husband's attention, Rebekah and Paul longed for their father's care. He was concerned that one or both of them would soon do something reckless to attract attention, and he prayed for God to heal them and fill the void left by their absent father.

With his immediate family covered, he quickly shifted his focus to praying for his cousins. As he mentioned James, he sensed an urge to see him and pray with him. He halted in his tracks, a frown creasing his brow as the compulsion intensified, tugging at him with an almost magnetic force.

He had grown up close to James, celebrating their birthdays together in their early years, as James was born on John Jr.'s first birthday. As they grew older, they drifted apart because they wanted different things. James wanted to be cool, while John Jr. just wanted to get good grades and make heaven. James attended church with his parents but was not a committed Christian and often made jokes about salvation.

But he would pray with him now he felt the urge to do so. As he crossed the road and walked toward his Aunt Elizabeth's house, he took out his mobile phone and called James. He wanted him to come out to meet him; he didn't want to go inside and see Aunt Elizabeth and get distracted from his mission.

"Can you bring yourself outside this instant? I'm standing in your driveway. I've come to say a prayer for you, sinner." He chuckled.

"John! What brings you here without an appointment?" James asked.

"You sound awfully self-important." John Jr. laughed. "Come on out. I told you; I've come to pray for you."

"How about you come inside?" James suggested. "I'm home alone with Andrew; he might get out of bed if he hears me trying to leave the house."

"Okay. I'm coming in." John Jr. approached the front door.

"Don't ring the bell. I'm coming down to open the door." James ended the call and raced down the stairs. He opened the door and stood back to let John Jr. in.

"Where's your jacket? It's a little chilly tonight," James said.

John Jr. shrugged. "I left home in a rush. I didn't think it would be so cold. It is summer, after all."

James rolled his eyes. "It's been four seasons today, John." He moved towards the kitchen. "Come in here; I'll make you a hot drink."

"Thank you." John followed him into the kitchen. "How come you're home alone with Andrew? I never thought I'd see the day Aunt Elizabeth would trust you to be responsible."

James paused as he was about to put the kettle on and gave John Jr. a warning look. "Another jibe at my ability to be responsible, and I will kick you out without that hot drink."

John Jr. exaggerated his shivering, trembling as if he were caught in a fierce snowstorm. "Oh, you wouldn't do that to your poor cousin, would you?"

James laughed and put the kettle on. "My mum's gone over to my dad's." He paused as he thought of how that sounded. He looked at John Jr. "That sounds weird, doesn't it?"

John Jr. shrugged as he took a seat at the breakfast bar. "Maybe in our grandparents' time."

James sighed. "I never thought I'd have to say that. I hope they get back together again."

"You can always pray. I pray a lot and have discovered that it makes a world of difference."

James looked at him before turning away to make their drinks. "I am not you, John."

"Who says you have to be?"

James placed a mug of hot chocolate before John Jr and sat next to him, wrapping his hands around his mug. "My mum would like me to be. She thinks you're perfect, perfect character, perfect grades."

"None of us is perfect. God helps me a great deal, and while I like to think it's because I pray a lot, it's really because He is good." John Jr. sipped his drink. "Thank you for this. I will remain in your debt for life."

James laughed. "You always talk like an old man."

John Jr. chuckled. "My mother would probably agree with you." He put his drink down and looked at James. "I saw you hanging out with Oliver Campbell and his mates at church a while back."

James sighed and looked away. "Yeah. That was a huge mistake." He sipped his drink.

John Jr. put his hand on James' shoulder and looked him in the eye. "Boys like Oliver Campbell never end well. And neither will those who hang out with them. Our friends will make or break us, and the Bible warns us against consenting when sinners entice us. It warns us to keep our foot from their path because their feet run to do evil."

James rubbed his face wearily. "Believe me, I know Oliver is bad news. At the time it seemed a good idea to hang out with him and his friends. Perhaps I wanted to belong and craved acceptance, or maybe I wanted to punish my mother by getting up to foolishness. Either way, I quickly learnt my lesson, and I won't be hanging out with him again. I assure you."

"Good," John Jr. said. "You need a new best friend. Jesus."

James grinned at his cousin. "You really did come here to pray for me, didn't you?"

"I told you I did."

"Okay. Why not? It's about time."

"Yes, it is," John Jr. said. "I don't mean to scare you, but death can come calling anytime. You want to live your life ready to make heaven."

James stared at him as he considered his words. "I guess you're right. Please pray for me."

"Place your right hand on your chest and repeat these words after me."

John Jr. appeared greatly relieved as he led James to the Lord inside his aunt's kitchen. It was almost as though a huge burden had been taken off his shoulders.

"Is that it?" James asked when the prayer was over.

"Yes," John Jr. said. "You are now born again, and now I know I will get to spend eternity with you in heaven."

James frowned. It was too soon to be talking about heaven, was it not? After all, they were young and had their whole lives ahead of them. He was going to voice his thoughts but changed his mind.

"Okay." He shrugged.

John Jr. drank his hot chocolate and set the mug down as he got ready to leave. James ran after him, grabbed his blue hooded jacket from the coat closet in the hallway, and handed it to him.

"Put this on and stay warm."

"Thanks." John Jr. slipped into the hooded jacket, which fit perfectly. "I'll have it cleaned and returned tomorrow."

"No worries. Thank you for the prayer. I feel like a new man already."

"Good." John Jr. said. "My work here is done. Now I can go home." He threw the hood over his head and stepped outside, shutting the door behind him.

Just then, Ava walked up to her living room window with a cup of tea in her hand. A furrow formed on her brows as she wondered where James was going. And if he was stepping out, who was home with Andrew? She noticed that Elizabeth had driven out about an hour ago, and since there was no car in the driveway, Elizabeth could not be back yet. She exhaled wearily.

James couldn't possibly be so reckless as to venture out and leave Andrew all alone, could he? The thought sent a chill down her spine.

She placed her cup of tea on the windowsill and reached for her mobile phone from the back pocket of her jeans, intending to call him. However, she paused when she noticed two young men in hoodies following closely behind him on an electric scooter. Her frown deepened. She had seen them earlier when Chris dropped her off. They rode past the front of Elizabeth's house, and something about them had been off. Possibly because they wore balaclava hoodies. She watched as they rode behind James, her heart caught in her throat as they intercepted him and got off their scooters.

"Oh no," she muttered softly, her heart racing in her chest as a man pulled out what appeared to be a knife. It all happened very quickly as she stood by the window, mouth and eyes wide open, watching helplessly as they cornered James, giving him no chance to escape and stabbing him continually.

Ava let out a piercing scream, her phone slipping from her grasp and clattering onto the floor with a loud thud as James fell to the ground on the sidewalk. As the assailants mounted their scooters and fled, she picked up her phone and, with tears in her eyes and a shaky hand, dialled the emergency services.

The next five minutes passed in a blur as she got dressed quickly. As soon as she heard a siren getting closer, she threw on her denim jacket and raced to the house, trying not to look towards the sidewalk. Frantically, she rang the bell, hoping and praying that Andrew would come to the door and let her in before anyone discovered he was home alone. She gasped in shock as the door opened, and James stood before her.

"You're here!" In relief, she grabbed him and hugged him even as she quickly pushed him into the house and shut the front door behind them.

"What's happening here?" James asked, his brow furrowing in confusion as he tried to make sense of her unpredictable behaviour.

"If you're here, who's lying on the sidewalk? Who was just stabbed, James? He came out of this house. He was wearing your hoodie; I thought he was you!"

James's eyes widened as he took a step back. "John! Oh my God!" He stepped towards the door, but Ava prevented him.

"Don't go! The police and ambulance are here. They'll help him. I called them thinking he was you."

"I need to call my mum."

"Where is she? I saw her drive out earlier."

"She's at my dad's. Someone needs to notify Uncle John and Aunt Victoria."

"Call your dad, and he can call them. You don't want to share this kind of news with your mum over the phone."

CHAPTER NINETEEN

Chris tried to remain calm as he listened to James and Ava explain that unknown assailants had stabbed John Jr. when he was leaving the house. The ambulance had taken him away; the police were still in the area. He had the responsibility of informing John.

He gazed at Elizabeth, nestled in the sheets of his bed, her form a captivating mess of tousled hair and soft fabric, a serene beauty caught in slumber. She was blissfully ignorant, and he wished he could leave her so. He did not wish to upset her, especially after how she had wept while he made love to her. He grimaced as he recalled he hadn't used protection, as he had none. How could he?

He had embraced celibacy once Elizabeth stopped sleeping with him, and he certainly hadn't planned to sleep with her tonight. Elizabeth wasn't on the pill, as far as he was aware. He shrugged; it was a problem for another time. He exited the room and entered the living room, calling John to pass on the message promptly. Then he returned to the bedroom to break the news to Elizabeth.

As he watched her sleep, he thought about what he had heard. Ava thought the person leaving the house was James. Was it possible the assailants also thought the same? Had the attack been planned for James, and John Jr. had only been at the wrong place at the wrong time, wearing the wrong attire?

How much of this was his fault? Was it possible his sins were still catching up with him? He had thought that with the collapse of his business empire, he was done paying for his mistakes. But what if he wasn't? What if vengeance was still going after him to take not only his marriage from him but his children, too? He could bear anything but that; anything as long as his boys were safe.

Elizabeth stirred and stretched languidly. "Hey," she said, stretching her hand to him, giving him her best come-hither look. "Come back to bed."

He slipped his phone into the pocket of his dressing gown and observed her, contemplating how to break the news. Sensing his resistance to return to bed, she sat up, pulling the sheet over her naked breasts and pushing her tousled hair out of her face.

"Are you okay?" she asked. "If you're worried about the boys, I can text Ava to go over."

"Ava is with the boys."

Misunderstanding him, she smiled and lay back against the pillows. "That was thoughtful of you." She patted the empty space beside her. "Come back to bed."

Chris inhaled deeply, the weight of the moment pressing down on him. "John Jr. was stabbed leaving the house. He's been taken to the hospital; no one knows the seriousness of his condition as yet or whether he's alive."

Elizabeth's eyes widened, and she turned pale as a sheet. She sat up slowly as if in a trance. Chris thought she would faint and moved closer to the bed.

"Are you okay, Elizabeth? Did you hear what I said?"

"Is he dead?" Her voice was a whisper.

Her heart raced as she tried to understand what Chris was saying. It was overwhelming, but her main concern was that he was alive. A part of her feared he might not be. She focused on Chris's lips, anticipating the unwanted words.

As Chris opened his mouth to speak, Elizabeth quickly shut her ears and squeezed her eyes tightly shut. She didn't want to hear it. Although she had asked, she wasn't ready for the answer.

"No!" She grabbed her hair with both hands. "He's dead, isn't he, Chris? John Jr.'s dead, isn't he?"

Chris sat on the edge of the bed and gently grasped her shoulders. "Elizabeth, please calm down. I can't say whether he's dead or not. I only know what I've been told. Ava saw him being stabbed. She thought he was James because he left the house wearing James' hoodie. She called the ambulance, dashed to the house, and discovered James was there. John Jr. has been removed from the scene and possibly taken to the nearest hospital. That's all I know."

"He might die."

Tears glistened in Elizabeth's eyes as Chris swiftly got off the bed, his movements a blur of urgency. He dressed quickly, a mix of concern and determination on his face, before helping her with her clothes, his touch both comforting and reassuring. She could not drive herself, so he put her in his car, and they drove to the house. As they got closer, they noticed the area where John Jr. had been stabbed was cordoned off by the police, causing Elizabeth to cry even more.

Chris led her into the house and escorted Ava to speak with the police. As the eyewitness who had called the emergency services, Ava was asked a series of questions, and her details were taken to enable the police to contact her in the future. Although the police officer was not going to give any information, the interaction revealed that John Jr. was taken from the scene unconscious. They returned to the house to relay the message to Elizabeth.

"I have to go to John now. He needs me. My poor brother." She burst out crying. "Chris, I feel like my whole world has fallen apart."

"I know. I know. It's going to be okay." Chris held her and stroked her hair.

James and Ava exchanged glances as they looked on. Elizabeth was the first to pull away.

"John and Victoria will be at the hospital now. We can go there. I'll drive you." Chris turned to Ava. "Can you watch James and Andrew? We might be gone a while."

"It's fine, Chris. I'll stay the night if I have to."

"Thank you, Ava. You're the best," Chris said as he ushered Elizabeth out of the house. "Be good, James."

James nodded. "You take care of Mum. Andrew and I will be fine."

Chris gave him a thumbs up and put his arm around Elizabeth's shoulder as he steered her out towards his car.

***

As John ended the call with Chris, his heart raced, and he tried to compose himself before breaking the news to Victoria. What was he going to tell her? He didn't know enough about the situation, but what he did know wasn't good. John Jr. had been stabbed. He would not have been if he had been home. It was all his doing, and Victoria was bound to be furious.

He decided to wait before telling her. He would visit the hospital to ascertain John Jr.'s condition and then inform her. As he stepped out of his home office into the hallway, Victoria rushed towards him from upstairs. She appeared unusually frantic as she took the winded stairs two at a time; he'd never seen her like that before.

John barely had a moment to gather his thoughts before she charged at him in a fit of rage, striking him again and again and yelling.

"This is for my son, you evil man! Son of Belial! Keeper of the vineyard of others! Hypocrite!"

He restrained her and held her to his chest as she wept uncontrollably.

"You drove him out. He had no reason to go out. You drove him out."

"Victoria, calm down. I promise you everything will be okay."

But she didn't want to be comforted by him, so she pushed him away and walked off.

"I need to go to my son. You and I are through, Pastor John. Go to your God, your church and the million women who need you because I don't. Not anymore."

Weeping silently, Victoria ran upstairs to her bedroom to throw some clothes on. She had just received the call every mother dreads. John Jr. had been stabbed in the streets. Her number had been found on his phone, and the paramedics had called her. She had no idea how bad his situation was, and she didn't know how she could go on living if anything happened to her baby.

She tried to pull herself together because she had to be strong now. Unlike the million women who had Pastor John to turn to in a crisis, she had only herself to depend on. But she wouldn't fail. She had been alone bearing her children and raising them; what did it matter now if she was alone with them in this dark hour?

She called Lindsay and gave instructions concerning Paul and Rebekah. They were to be told John had been taken to the hospital, and she had gone to be with him, but they were not to be told the extent of his injuries. She didn't want them panicking, especially as she was not home to comfort them.

As she walked out of the house, John stood by his car, holding the door open for her. She ignored him and got behind the wheel of her car, starting it and pulling out of the driveway while he looked at her in bewilderment.

***

"Are you in love with him? With Pastor John? I saw your pictures online and how you looked at him. I also noticed how you looked at him when he came to pray for Daisy."

Barry couldn't shake the curiosity that bubbled within him about Mabel's unwavering devotion to Pastor John. What was it about the man that inspired such loyalty? He felt compelled to delve deeper into her feelings and uncover the mystery behind this steadfast admiration.

After leaving Elizabeth, he had come straight to Mabel's home and joined Mabel and the girls for dinner. The meal had been delicious, but he hadn't come over for a meal. It was time he knew where he stood. Mabel had rebuffed every move he'd made at a reconciliation. In Paris, he tried to make the trip about her as much as the girls, taking her out at night when the girls were exhausted from the day's activities in Disney and fast asleep. And while she'd happily let him wine and dine her, when they returned to their hotel, she went to bed. Alone.

Apart from the night at his house when she'd let him kiss her, she had denied all physical contact, and he was dying. He reckoned she'd succumbed to that kiss to remind him of what he had and give him a foretaste of what was to come. But sometimes, she acted so aloof he didn't know what to think anymore. He concluded her indifference to him was because another man was in her life. So far, he knew only of Pastor John.

Mabel closed the curtains and faced Barry, giving him a smile that was both sweet and sad. She'd thought she loved Pastor John, but now she knew better. "No." She shook her head. "I'm not in love with him, but I was infatuated. Very much so."

Her answer hit Barry with the force of a freight train, leaving him utterly stunned. "Why?"

Mabel furrowed her well-shaped brows as she pondered the question. After a minute, she shrugged. "What can I say? He's good-looking, dresses well, saved my life, was great with the girls, and made time for us."

Barry took a moment, nodding thoughtfully as he carefully dissected her words, seeking to understand their deeper meaning. "So, in other words, you're saying you want a man who's attractive, stylish, makes time for you and the girls and invests in you?"

"Yes, I guess." With a nonchalant shrug, she strolled over to the sofa and settled into the cushions.

"Do you believe I was or am that man?"

A hint of a smile played on her lips as she studied Barry. "I find you attractive, Barry. You know that. You're very stylish. In the beginning, you were a great husband and dad and spent time with the girls and me, but later on, we saw more of your money and less of you, and then you were out of our lives, and we saw only your money."

"But you needed me to be there."

"Yes. Pastor John was there every time I needed him." Mabel's gaze drifted, and her eyes glistened with unshed tears as a wave of emotion washed over her.

Barry took a step towards her. "Mabel, I'm back, and I won't leave you or the girls again. You have my promise."

Mabel let out a hollow laugh, a sound tinged with sorrow as she wiped away her tears. "This is the problem! You promised not to leave me when we married. But you lost interest in me. I was overweight, not going to school, and couldn't do anything right. You complained all the time. I know I embarrassed you. You wanted a wife you could show off to the world, and I wasn't that person. I get that. But to just get up and leave the way you did. That was cruel, Barry. How can I trust you again? How do I know that if I let you back in, you won't find some excuse to leave again?"

Barry went on his knees. "I'm not the man I was when I walked away from you, Mabel. Please believe that. I made a huge mistake and don't need to be told I was a fool. Please, believe me. I won't walk away again."

"And if I put on weight?" she asked.

It was a legitimate question. Barry understood her fears. He may have struggled to answer that question a few weeks ago, but not now that he spent a great deal of time listening to Pastor John's messages. A few days ago, he had listened to a message from last year's men's conference and understood where he had erred.

He had complained about Mabel without realising it was his responsibility as a husband to make her the type of woman he desired. Pastor John made that clear when he spoke to men at the conference about cultivating their gardens. The preacher likened the wife to a garden and said it was up to the husband to make of her what he wished her to be.

"I don't want you to put on any more weight, not just because you're more beautiful this way, but also because your health is important to me. But, if you did, I wouldn't walk away. I realise now that I was taking the easy way out by walking away. You're my wife and it is my responsibility to make you better. So, I will go with you to the gym, and we will stay in shape together as a couple.

"And if you stopped going to school? Then I'll enrol on the course, and we'll go to school together. What else do you want to know? Oh, how about if you abandoned your business? We'll do that together, too. Things are not going to be as they were before. I plan to make things better. Make us better. I am intentional about us having a great life together and what I need to do to make that happen. What other doubts do you have?"

Mabel lowered her head as the tears streamed down her cheeks in quiet despair. As if drawn by an invisible thread, Barry stood up and made his way towards her, his heart aching to offer comfort amidst her sorrow.

"Oh, baby." He picked her up and sat on the sofa, cradling her in his arms. "I love you. I never stopped. Everything I did, every penny I gave, even when I walked away, was because I didn't want you to lack anything. I provided for you because I love you. I couldn't remarry, try as I might. No one was good enough, and though I had several reasons for rejecting them, I rejected them mainly because they weren't you. They weren't the mother of my children. Deep inside, it was you I wanted."

He kissed her tears, and when he reached her lips, they parted in anticipation. The kiss they shared was explosive. He picked her up and carried her to her bedroom, hoping the girls who were in Tracy's room watching a movie after dinner and before bedtime would not see them. Fortunately, they made it into Mabel's bedroom without being noticed, and as he shut the door behind them and put her down, she was all over him, trying to get him out of his clothes.

A while later, Barry propped up on his elbow to watch Mabel sleep. She was so beautiful, so perfect for him. How had he not seen it before? As if she sensed he watched her, she opened her eyes, a smile gracing her lips at the sight of him.

"Hi."

Barry returned her smile. "Hi."

She pulled his head down for a kiss. "I missed you."

"I missed you more." He meant it. No other woman compared to Mabel. For him, she was home. Besides, her newfound confidence extended to the bedroom, and her unprecedented boldness captivated him.

"Can we talk about getting married again?"

"Later." She shoved him back against the pillows, sprawling over him. "Much later."

Their lips met in a lingering kiss, lasting a few minutes before Barry pulled away. "I think we should discuss it now." He moved, so she was lying on her back, and he wrapped his arm around her waist and pulled her close. "I don't know about you, but I don't want to carry on having sex with someone I'm not married to."

Mabel burst into laughter, but her amusement faded as she noticed the earnest look in Barry's eyes.

"I realise I'm not in a position to make any demands, and I'm making none. You were mine, and in my arrogance, I let you go. But I want to come back home, Mabel. My desire is to be your husband once more and reside at home. I don't want to sneak around and slip into your bed unnoticed while the girls are not watching."

Mabel giggled as she realised that was what had just happened, and this time, Barry joined in her laughter.

"I don't want that either."

"Then let's get married again," he urged. "We can fly out to Lagos, have a traditional marriage ceremony and a big party before the summer holiday ends. I'm sure the girls would love the experience of spending a week or two in Lagos."

"It sounds like a plan. But I want more than a traditional marriage ceremony this time."

"Tell me what you want. Anything. I'll give it to you."

Gently touching his face, Mabel gazed into his eyes. "I want to get married in a civil ceremony. I want to know that you can't just get up, walk out, return the bride price, and we are done."

Barry tightened his grip around her waist. "I will never walk out on you again. You have my word. But I'm happy to give you whatever you want. You call the shots; I'll marry you in every country on the planet if you like."

"Thank you, but a traditional marriage ceremony in Lagos and a civil marriage ceremony in London will suffice." She kissed him. "And I want a honeymoon. I didn't have one the last time."

Barry flinched. He didn't want to consider how he had taken her for granted. "You'll get your honeymoon anywhere you want, my darling. Your wish is my command."

"Good man." Mabel framed his face and kissed him.

Satisfied that he had her again, Barry made love to her the second time that evening. It was unrushed, as he loved every inch of her body. When they were done, he looked into her eyes and knew without a doubt that he held her heart again. He lifted her hand to his lips and kissed it, a silent promise to her and himself that he would treasure it, be careful with it and not break it this time.

They got out of bed to shower, and Mabel reached for her phone as it beeped. "It's a text message from Pastor John."

Not Pastor John again!

Barry glanced at the digital alarm clock on the bedside table. It was 9:15 p.m.

What did the man want?

"What does he want?" he asked.

"Oh my God!" Mabel discarded the phone, reacting as if it had scorched her. "This is dreadful news."

"What is it?" Barry asked as he walked over to where the phone lay and picked it up. He read the text. Pastor John asked the whole church to join him in a prayer vigil for his son, who was stabbed earlier that evening.

He put the phone down on the bedside table and hugged Mabel, using his thumbs to brush away the tears rolling down her cheeks. "It's okay, baby. Don't cry. I'm sure the young man will be fine. Do you want to go for this vigil?"

She nodded. "Pastor John's been there for us the last year and never asked for anything in return. It's the least I can do."

"I agree," Barry said. "We'll go together. Go and have a shower, and I'll find the nanny's number on your phone and ask her to come and stay overnight with the girls."

Under the shower's spray, silent tears streamed down Mabel's face. She couldn't believe it. John Jr. had been stabbed. How did such a thing happen to a man like Pastor John? If such a thing could happen to him, and if he lost his son, what hope was there for people like her who were lesser mortals?

She was glad Barry was around to take charge because she felt completely ineffective. He rushed her out of the shower and helped her get dressed, and by the time they were ready, the nanny had arrived to stay with the girls for the night.

"Thank you for coming with me," she said as they entered his car, and he started the engine.

He smiled and stroked her cheek. "I could never leave you to go alone," he said as he pulled out of the driveway. "Besides, he's my pastor now."

CHAPTER TWENTY

As John drove through the double wrought-iron gates of The Vine Church, he saw that the lights in the main church auditorium were on. Someone had flung open the double oak doors on all four entrances, and the ushers were preparing the hall for the emergency vigil service he had called.

The four car parks outside the four major entrances to the building were fast filling up with cars. Some parishioners walked through the gates on foot; others alighted from their cars and taxis. All looked mournful, and many wept as they walked towards the church doors.

John drove past the building towards the church administrative block behind. Pulling: Pulling his vehicle into the parking spot in front of the building reserved for pastors, he brought it to a halt and climbed out. Before the night vigil, he needed some solitude, and he was thankful he could make it to his office, encountering no one but Liam, who wisely remained silent at his desk.

Sitting in his chair, he buried his head in his hands. In turmoil, he tried to pray. Everything that had happened that day flashed before his eyes. His anger at Alan's interference in his marriage and family life. His quarrel with Victoria because she invited Alan into their affairs which led to him hitting his son for daring to speak the truth. Yes, he had neglected his family while he helped other families. In his attempt to be a good shepherd, he failed to care for his family. Victoria and the kids came first, but he had not prioritised them.

He had left his responsibilities with Victoria as he cared for the church members and had not even supported her as she tried her best. When she complained, he shut her down. Her going to Alan annoyed him, but she went to his mentor because she believed he wouldn't listen to her. And he had given her reasons to believe that. He loved his wife very much, even if he was useless in showing it. As great as he was telling others what to do and knowing how others ought to sort out their problems, he was futile regarding his personal affairs. To heed Alan, speak with his wife, and try to grasp her complaints would have shown wisdom. Then, John Jr. wouldn't have been a vulnerable target on the streets.

The arrival at the hospital, as they wheeled his unconscious, intubated son into surgery, was a harrowing experience for him. He stood there, paralysed and wishing he could undo his mistakes. Victoria was inconsolable but wouldn't allow him to comfort her. She was determined to be independent, and he couldn't blame her. But she needed someone even if it wasn't him, so he called Alan, and as the older man arrived, he heard God's instruction to leave the hospital and go to church to pray all night.

You can't do anything for him here. Go to Zion. I will meet you there.

Taking out his phone, he messaged as many members as possible, requesting they forward the message and gather at the church for a vigil. As their pastor had been there for them all in their time of need and asked that they be there for him in his hour of need. A laugh almost escaped him. He had always thought himself to be above a need.

As the door opened, he looked up to see Alan enter, his expression far more sombre than John had ever witnessed. As he rose to his feet, he saw Victoria behind. His heart quickened in its pace. She didn't look at him as she entered, and Alan shut the door behind them. She hung by the door, wrapping her arms around herself.

Pastor Alan cleared his throat as he approached John's desk. "John, I'll be here for the vigil and help in any capacity you require me to."

John nodded. He couldn't trust himself to speak when his throat appeared constricted. Alan looked over his shoulder to where Victoria remained by the door and then back at John.

"You and Victoria need to talk."

As he opened the door to leave, Pastor Tom stood on the other side and quickly looked in.

"Would you like me to start the service?" he asked.

"Start the opening prayers and worship. Victoria and I will be out soon."

Pastor Tom nodded and retreated, and Pastor Alan turned to John. "I'll go with Tom and see where I can help." He patted Victoria gently on the shoulder as he left the office, shutting the door behind him.

John pressed the buzzer, and Liam entered the office promptly. "I'm with my wife and do not wish to be disturbed."

Liam looked surprised but nodded. "Yes, of course, Pastor John." He retreated as quickly as he had entered, glancing briefly at Victoria before shutting the door behind him.

John walked up to Victoria and noticed for the first time that she looked drained. She didn't resist or flinch as he picked her up in his arms and carried her to the sofa in the corner of his office. He sat down and held her in his lap, his arms wrapped around her.

"I'm sorry. I truly am. I can't tell you how much," he whispered.

After a long silence, Victoria spoke, but her words weren't what John expected. "Your apology means nothing to me, John. All that matters to me right now is my son. I want my baby, John. I want my baby."

John felt gutted as he watched her cry. He understood Victoria's patience with him had run out. The woman who had once loved and admired him had grown resentful and now didn't care. She wept not because of him or the apparent problems in their marriage but because of her son. John Jr. was all that mattered to her right now. If John Jr. died or failed to make a full recovery, Victoria would never forgive or return to him. She wouldn't even remain physically in a bid to keep up appearances. She would leave, taking Rebekah and Paul with her.

When she turned to Alan, that should have been a hint that she was done. That was God warning him to go home and put things right. But he hadn't listened. He let his ego instead of God's spirit lead him, and here he was, his son was lying on an operating table, fighting for his life; his wife was broken as he'd never seen her and his life as he knew it was about to be over.

He knew how to rectify the situation, but how did he pray to God when the situation with Victoria blocked his access to God? He let her cry, holding her and stroking her hair, thankful she didn't push him away as she had done earlier at the hospital.

"It is going to be okay, I promise. I know you don't believe that, but it will be okay."

Victoria cried until she had no more strength left. She had come with Alan because she had a small ray of hope that God would hear when John prayed. For all of John's faults, he was a man respected because he had results when he prayed. She longed for her son and would do anything to get him back.

Her eyes pleaded as she looked up at him. "I need you to bring him back home to me."

"I know. But I can't bring him back home. Only God can."

Victoria shook her head. "Don't tell me that, Pastor John. For years, I've witnessed your miraculous work. I need a miracle now."

"I need a miracle, too. He's my son too. But God works miracles, and I can't talk to Him, not with this situation between us."

Victoria slid off his lap and moved to sit at the other end of the sofa. "I am listening."

"Why did you marry me?"

Victoria was utterly astonished by John's question. "John, I don't see how this is relevant; my son is in hospital, and his life hangs in the balance; how is this ridiculous question going to help?"

John remained silent, intently watching his wife as he prayed for her cooperation. A minute later, a weary sigh escaped her lips, her shoulders slumping.

"I married you because I love you."

"What was it about me that you loved?"

"I loved that you were handsome, studying to be a doctor, you were celibate, and keeping yourself for marriage, and all the girls wanted you." She shrugged and looked away.

"What has changed?" he asked. "What has brought you to the place where you no longer love me and wish to end our marriage?"

"You're asking this, John?"

"Humour me."

"I hate that you ignore me. I feel like you don't see me, except when you want sex or want a whipping post because the children haven't lived up to your expectations.

You spend much time with other women, especially single mothers, fixing their issues, while you expect me to fix the same issues you won't let them fix. I won't live like that anymore, John. I'm done."

"Is that all? Or is there more?" John asked quietly.

"That's the problem in a nutshell. I'm done living like a woman without a husband while my husband takes care of women abandoned by their husbands." she paused and continued. "And given your uninhibited interactions, I'm surprised they aren't smitten with you and seeking a deeper connection. In front of me, Mabel has the nerve to tie your shoelaces, and later, she cooks you lunch—like she's your wife. That's too much, John. If I offered comforting hugs to the male members of our church, how would you react? Or imagine you walked in and saw a pastor kneeling to tie my shoelaces or sandals. If I were invited to lunch by a pastor or a church brother for ministry, what then?"

John's gaze fixed on his wife as she spoke. For the first time, a new perspective began to unfold before him. If Victoria got that close to another man, he would hurt somebody. The mere thought of it was already causing his blood to boil. He would have to review his commitment to the flock. He had to be able to serve them without destroying his own family.

"You're right," he said after a while.

Surprised, Victoria turned to look at him. "What was that?" Surely, she hadn't heard him right. Was John agreeing with her and not accusing her of being selfish and self-centred?

"You're right," he repeated. "I could never quietly watch you do the things you've just mentioned with another man, and I see now the error of my ways and how I've hurt you continually through the years. I am truly sorry, and I can change, and I will change and be a better husband and a better father."

Victoria looked at him, her eyes welling with tears. "You're a good man, John, and I know you do the things you do out of the goodness of your heart, and I am not asking you not to help anyone, but I want to know that I matter, John and that I will get your best, not your crumbs after you've satisfied everyone else. And I want to work with you, by your side, not left at home like there are sections of your life that I can't fit into. If I don't know anything, I want to learn. When you dismiss me and shut me out of your work, that hurts. It's like you have this life I'm not a part of and where I'm not welcome."

John nodded as he acknowledged he had made a serious mistake. It would take a miracle for Victoria to stay with him after tonight, especially if John Jr. didn't survive.

"I've wronged you, and I'm sorry. I have no justification, only regret, and I hope you can forgive me. Victoria, I need your support, not only tonight as we pray for our son, but every day. My life is incomplete without you, and I love you so much. You have my word that I will change everything that makes you unhappy; nothing will be the same from now on."

The tears fell silently as Victoria looked at her husband. She knew she could trust him. John did not give his word carelessly. "This one time," she told him. "But if nothing changes, I'm gone. Do you understand?"

John nodded and reached out to take her hand. "God answers me when I pray. He's never failed me. I will pray for our son, Victoria, but I need your assurance that whatever the morning brings, and whichever way God answers me, you will remain by my side."

Victoria wept some more as the import of John's words dawned on her, reminding her of the gravity of the situation before them. They may very well be planning to bury their son in the morning. John held her hand and let her cry, and then she raised her head and looked him in the eye.

"You have my assurance that whatever the morning brings, and whichever way God answers you, I will remain by your side."

John let out a sigh of relief as he pulled her off the sofa and onto his lap again, holding her as if his life depended on it.

CHAPTER TWENTY-ONE

Half an hour later, John and Victoria joined the service. With the choir singing "Tis so sweet to trust in Jesus," the worship session was in full swing. The worship leader had tears streaming down his face.

Packed like a Sunday service, the church auditorium was full. Worshippers lifted their hands and eyes to the Lord, fully engaged in the atmosphere of praise and devotion. As the worship ended, John stood to his feet and turned to Victoria, his hand stretched towards her. She was surprised but quickly recovered as she placed her hand in his and allowed him to pull her to her feet. Her legs wobbled slightly as she walked beside John to the pulpit. He wrapped his arm around her and pulled her tightly to his side. Together, they faced the congregation that had gathered to keep vigil and pray for their son.

"Good evening, brethren," John said. "My wife and I would like to thank everyone for taking time out of their busy schedules to stand with us in prayer through the night for our son. We can't begin to tell you how grateful we are. I'm sure Victoria has a word for you all."

Victoria turned to look at him wide-eyed, but his gentle smile and the look in his eyes assured her she could do it.

"Like John said, we are immensely grateful to you all for coming tonight. We know you all had plans, and this was not how you expected to spend your evening, and we are overwhelmed by your show of love. Thank you."

With pleading eyes, she looked up at him, silently begging to return to her seat. He nodded, leaned in, and gave her a soft kiss on her lips. The congregation burst into an eruption of joy. Victoria felt a rush of warmth flood her cheeks, turning the colour of a ripe crimson as she pivoted on her heels. With a grace that masked her embarrassment, she walked back to her seat, each step a careful balance of dignity and fluster.

John lifted his hand, and the eruption began to subside. "Tonight, before any prayers, I will guide the congregation toward repentance. John Jr. is in hospital, having suffered multiple stab wounds. God may choose to let him remain with us or call him away from this world. If we were called away today, where would we go? Please ponder this question for the next few minutes, and if you need to surrender your life to Jesus or rededicate your life to Him, come out and repent before the altar."

John turned to Tom and signalled for him to continue as he, to the surprise of the entire church, left the pulpit and knelt before the altar. He, more than anyone else, needed to repent before the Lord. He had not been a good husband or father, so he had not been a good minister nor brought glory to God.

"Father, I repent of my sins; of preaching one thing and practising another. I am sorry for disregarding those you sent to guide me, and I acknowledge I was prideful and arrogant, and I ask for your mercy and forgiveness. You have called this meeting; the congregation has gathered to join Victoria and me in praying for our son. Please intervene, Lord, that he may live, not for my sake. Whether he lives or dies, I am your servant and will serve you faithfully until I draw my last breath. But I ask that he live for your namesake, that the world will see and hear what you have done, and sinners will be converted and come to Christ, in Jesus' name. Amen."

Victoria rose from her seat and made her way over to John. She knelt beside him, gently taking his hand in hers, their fingers intertwining in a moment that felt both fragile and unbreakable. Now, it was necessary to seek the Lord's forgiveness. She spent years criticising John for his neglect and flaws, while ignoring her own. Her obsession with John and her desperation to marry him had informed her decision to be born again. She had never truly converted and harboured bitterness toward God for the time John spent away from her.

"Lord, I admit I haven't known you nor desired to. I only wanted John. You gave John to me, but when I had him, you no longer mattered. The gift meant more to me than the giver, so I never truly had John. Now, I see everything clearly. I repent and ask for your mercy and forgiveness." As Victoria began to cry, John let go of her hand, put his arm around her, and kissed her forehead.

The congregation was amazed as they watched their beloved pastor, and his wife kneel before the altar. Many congregants wept openly as they poured their hearts out in prayer amidst the gentle singing in the background, the weight of the moment enveloping the church in a profound sense of reverence and raw emotion.

Elizabeth and Chris sat together in the front row. Both wore solemn expressions; Elizabeth looked pale, leaning on Chris. Mabel and Barry arrived shortly and seated themselves in the front row across the aisle from Elizabeth and Chris. Elizabeth lifted her head abruptly, her heart racing as she nearly leapt from her seat in shock. Her mind registered the name Barry, and though her mouth opened to echo it, her vocal cords refused to cooperate.

What was he doing here?

His companion looked familiar; Elizabeth felt she'd seen her before. Did they belong to The Vine Church, or were they just at the vigil? She quickly regained her composure as Barry briefly acknowledged her with a nod. He took Mabel's hand, and mirroring the gesture, Elizabeth grasped Chris's hand. Unaware of what was transpiring, Chris wrapped his other arm around her, pulling her close and kissing her forehead.

Elizabeth glanced at Barry and then at Chris. It was the first time she had seen both men together, and she berated herself for her foolishness. Next to the kind and gentle Chris, Barry looked ruthless, and she recognised one as selfless and the other as selfish. She must have been mad to want a man willing to leave his wife and children to be with her. How could she not have known that he would deal with her just as maliciously? Chris would never do that to her. She was relieved that her relationship with Barry had come to an end. His ex-wife was more than welcome to have him back in her life if she wanted.

Elizabeth wished them well and hoped that she had not completely ruined her chances with Chris.

She edged closer, and he turned to meet her gaze, intrigued by the sudden proximity. "Are you all right?" he asked in a whisper. Maintaining eye contact, she offered a slight smile and a nod.

When Mabel observed Pastor John kneeling at the altar, head bowed, and shoulders slumped, she felt sympathy for him. He seemed broken and unlike the invincible man she once believed him to be. As she reflected on her feelings of gratitude towards him, a thought nagged at her—he wasn't all that different from Barry after all. Even though he never truly stepped away from home, he continually turned his back on his family, prioritising the needs of others over those closest to him.

She questioned his wife's emotional state when other women summoned him, and he hastened to them as if they all shared him. She could never tolerate that. Thankful for the man God had given her, she squeezed Barry's hand. As he turned to look at her, his love for her was evident, and she smiled up at him, grateful for a new beginning.

In one of the pews at the back of the church, Rebekah sat beside Paul and Lindsay, her heart fluttering as she watched her parents kneel solemnly before the altar. Tears welled in her eyes, blurring her vision. She remained dazed, grappling with her brother's ordeal. As the tears fell, she brushed them away, pulled out her phone, and sent Conor a quick message.

I can't continue to see you. I'm rededicating my life to Jesus tonight.

She didn't have to wait long for a response; one arrived almost immediately.

Is this a joke? I understand that you're feeling emotional right now because your brother's in hospital. You can have as much space as you need to heal. I'll wait even longer than September to have sex.

Rebekah shook her head as she texted a short reply.

Goodbye, Conor.

This time, she didn't wait for a reply; she switched off her phone and walked to the altar, finding space behind her parents and kneeling with her head bowed.

"Dear Lord, I come before you with a humble and contrite heart. I'm not going to deny what I did since you already know. I'm so, so sorry. Please don't let John Jr. die," she pleaded. "If you save him, I will dedicate my life to serving you, but I need my brother with me to hold my hand and guide me in a closer walk with you. Please."

Standing at the pulpit, Pastor Tom glanced around the auditorium and called out, "Who else is coming to the altar to surrender their lives to Christ or to renew their commitment to Him?"

In the background, the choir continued to sing, "I need you, oh, I need you, every hour I need you, oh, bless me now, my saviour, I come to thee."

As Elizabeth watched parishioners begin to leave their seats en masse, she gently pulled away from Chris's embrace, stood tall, and confidently approached the altar. Kneeling beside her brother, she lovingly rested a hand on his shoulder.

"Lord, it's me, Elizabeth. My parents were missionaries and loved you. My father led me to Christ as a little girl. As I grew older, my rebellion created an increasingly large divide between us. My greed caused me to be unfaithful to my husband, consequently harming him, my marriage, and my children. The lust of the flesh, eyes, and the pride of life ruled me. What can I say? I am a sinner.

"But I do not desire to continue in sin. As I struggle against my own shortcomings, I yearn for your forgiveness and seek your saving embrace. The thought of Chris discovering my actions and divorcing me is unbearable. And I can't accept the possibility of my brother losing his son. If my parents did one thing well in serving you, I urge you to hear my petition for me and my brother to bring healing to our lives, marriages, and families."

Elizabeth brushed a tear from her cheek, her heart heavy with emotion. She squeezed John's shoulder, offering him both comfort and a silent connection in that poignant moment.

An arm wrapped around her waist, pulling her close. She looked up and saw Chris on his knees beside her. As she smiled at him through tear-filled eyes, she wondered how she had taken this good man for granted. Once again, she prayed that God would save her marriage. The thought of a future without Chris was too much for her.

Chris bowed his head in reflection as he considered Biobele. Slim, tall, and very dark-skinned, she embodied the African queen. She spent a considerable amount of time in his home in Port-Harcourt, preparing meals for him and attending to his intimate needs. He paid her generously, but their arrangement was short-lived as she'd married. Doubra, her younger sister, quickly replaced her as the pay was good. He had not intended for that arrangement to extend to the bedroom, but it had for eighteen months.

Then he returned to work in Port Harcourt after visiting his family in the UK, and Alaere was in the kitchen cooking instead of Doubra. She explained that Doubra had married while he was away in London and that she would be cooking his meals in Doubra's stead. He had known where it was leading and should have refused. But he didn't because, though much older, Alaere's beauty and sensuality captivated him, and so he let her cook his meals and bedded her until the incident at the David-West site that killed her husband, his friend, Alabo. An incident that had been his fault, fuelled by his greed.

"Lord, forgive me for falling short of your expectations for me. My past holds shameful secrets I can't reveal to Elizabeth or my sons. Your unseen influence made me wealthy, yet my affluence led to unspeakable acts. Alabo trusted me, but I betrayed him by having an affair with his wife and daughters because of my financial status, which they found alluring.

"My greed led me to alter the David-West Tower's building plan, bribing officials to approve an unsafe design. Almost one hundred people perished, and I will always bear the weight of their deaths. I kneel at your altar, acknowledging that I have sinned against you. I seek your forgiveness and implore you to shield my wife and children from the avenger of blood."

As Barry approached the altar, he was careful to kneel as far away from Elizabeth and Chris as possible. His observation of Elizabeth with Chris brought her marital status to mind. However disintegrated her marriage had been when they met, Elizabeth had been married, and for over a year, he'd had an affair with another man's wife. How could he expect to remarry Mabel and have a happy home with a sin like that hanging over his head? He bowed his head in an act of contrition.

"Father, I acknowledge I am not worthy to kneel before your altar or offer prayers to you. I left my family for another man's wife, destroying his home and family. Aware of my transgressions, I humbly request your mercy and pardon.

He glanced up at a sudden movement, smiling as Mabel intertwined her fingers with his. With a delicate touch, she reached up with her free hand and softly wiped away the tear that had slipped down his cheek. With her eyes locked on his, she smiled back and then bowed her head.

"Lord Jesus, I need you. When I look in the mirror, I don't like the woman I see. I am a manipulative woman who tried to seduce a man of God and cause him to sin against you and his wife. With even a little encouragement, I would've had an affair; my desire for another woman's husband was that strong. I longed for Victoria Griffith's husband and yearned for the life she led, and only now do I realise just how twisted those desires truly were. Please show me your mercy and forgive my transgressions. Help me in my journey to deepen my faith and strengthen my role as a wife and mother, even as I seek to grow and become the best version of myself."

A wave of people gracefully moved toward the altar, each step filled with anticipation and a sense of purpose. Pastor Ben Nkosi rose from his seat at the back of the church, and with hands clasped and head bowed, he walked towards the altar. He was still suspended from his pastoral duties and had stayed away from church not only out of shame but also out of pride, secret resentment, and rebellion.

Hearing about John Jr.'s stabbing affected him deeply, and as he came to pray tonight with his church family, he realised he had no reason to feel anger. He had sinned, and it was time to acknowledge that and stop feeling resentful over his suspension. Walking alongside him, his wife Gloria linked her fingers through his as a perfect reflection of their love. Gloria was still with him despite everything, and he squeezed her hand gently as he silently gave thanks.

Georgieta looked up as she approached the altar and noticed Mariatu, who was scanning the crowded area for a place to kneel. As the two women gazed into each other's eyes, the world around them seemed to disappear. After a heartbeat of hesitation, Georgieta stepped forward, wrapping her arms around Mariatu in a warm embrace.

"My sister, I forgive you," she said, bringing a smile to Mariatu's face. Side-by-side, they prayed before the altar.

Audrey Campbell stepped forward with tears glistening in her eyes, her heart pounding as she approached the altar. Each step felt heavy with emotion as she thought of John Jr. fighting for his life. His stabbing reminded her of the frailty of life, and not for the first time since she arrived for the vigil did she ask herself where she would be if death came calling suddenly. With a sense of reverence, she bowed gracefully before the altar.

"Father, I humbly seek your mercy and grace. I have led the women in this church for years, but I haven't quite walked the talk. My husband sees my hypocrisy, and for this reason, he has rejected you and the church. Where my children are concerned, I have also failed, yet I constantly pass judgement on other wives and mothers. Forgive me, Lord."

With her head bowed and a heavy heart, tears cascaded down her cheeks, each one a testament to the deep sorrow that wrapped around her like a shroud.

"Brethren, the altar area is full. If you'd like to dedicate or rededicate your life to Christ, please stand or kneel where you are," Pastor Tom said.

At the back of the church, in the last pew by the north entrance, Oliver Campbell watched with a sneer as people who could not reach the already crowded altar knelt or stood by their seats. A smirk played on his lips as he observed them. The lady to his left stood with both hands clasped between her breasts, her head titled up; she sobbed and prayed and sang in tune with the choir. "Just as I am, without one plea, but that thy blood was shed for me, and that thou bidd'st me come to thee, O Lamb of God, I come, I come."

"Pretenders," he muttered under his breath. "The lot of them."

He had been a member of The Vine Church for many years and understood that the congregation was far from righteous. Tonight, they would pour out their hearts to God, shedding tears of remorse, only to awaken the next morning and slip back into their familiar patterns.

Feeling disgusted, he stood and walked out of the church. It was time he went home. Tonight wasn't a good night to meet his gang in church. And James David-West remained an issue that needed to be resolved. His guys had failed to get the snitch.

James had been avoiding him, and he figured it was because he had told on him. Pastor John had asked his mother if he was giving drugs to young people at church. That had confirmed his suspicion. He decided to teach James a lesson, but there had been a mix-up, and John Jr. had been stabbed instead. Not that he was sorry. John Jr. was the preacher's son, and if the preacher chose to meddle in his affairs, it was only fitting that his son faced consequences.

His phone rang, and he paused on the church steps and pulled it from his pocket. It was one of his team members who had been assigned to take out James.

"How's it going?" he asked, slipping a hand in his pocket as he listened to the younger boy apologising for the mix-up.

"We really thought it was him, man," he said. "He came out of the house wearing the jacket we've seen him wear many times. We were close when we realised who it was, and the prissy boy had seen our faces as he pulled at the balaclava, so we had to finish up."

"Let's not discuss this again. We need to move forward and re-strategise. Hopefully, goody-two-shoes won't live to tell the police anything. Lie low for a while and stay away from church."

He ended the call and put the phone back in his pocket. As he walked down the steps into the car park, a car pulled up, and three people got out. He paused as he recognised James walking towards the church. A young lady walked behind him and pulled Andrew behind her. He looked at James as the woman bowed slightly to speak to Andrew. He made a finger-gun hand gesture and laughed satisfactorily as James froze to the spot, and fear filled his face.

"Be very afraid, James," he muttered under his breath. No one insulted him and got away with it, and James's failure to deliver or return the drugs, coupled with his betrayal, was viewed by him as a grave insult.

He exited the church premises, pausing by the gates to light a cigarette before continuing his journey towards the train station. As he journeyed home by train, he pushed thoughts of James David-West out of his mind. James would get what was coming to him. His men would strike again once this situation had blown over and the police had ended their investigation. He turned his mind to other matters, such as the hit his older brother, Freddie, had ordered on a drug dealer.

If Freddie's men were successful, they would walk away from the dealer's house with about a quarter of a million pounds in drugs and cash. He chuckled, a glint of mischief in his eyes as he rubbed his hands together eagerly. Freddie had offered him a huge sum to keep his share until he got out of prison, and he couldn't wait to get his hands on the money. He planned to fly out to the Caribbean on holiday following the hit in a couple of days. It would be a summer like no other.

He travelled four stops on the train and exited the train and the station. As he walked down the street leisurely to his parents' home, he lit another cigarette, his mind filled with the holiday ahead of him. He reached home and paused outside the little pedestrian gate to finish his cigarette. Someone called his name as he threw the cigarette butt to the ground and crushed it underfoot. He froze with one hand on the little gate. He had not heard that voice in a long time, and it couldn't be him. Could it be? He was still in prison; he must be.

Feeling for his penknife in his jogger's pockets, Oliver turned around slowly, and it was just as he had feared. His nemesis, a top member of a rival gang, stood before him, a small gun in hand.

When had he been released from prison? Oliver wondered.

"This is for my time in prison, Oliver Campbell," he said, releasing the trigger.

EPILOGUE

John Jr. glanced briefly in the direction of his parents as he climbed the altar to share his testimony. It had been two months since God saved him from death. He was grateful to be alive, and for two months, he had anticipated this moment to share with the people of God what had transpired that night.

His parents smiled at him, and he looked away as his dad reached out to hold hands with his mum. He was still getting used to their public displays of affection. While he liked their new relationship, he sometimes thought they overdid it.

Pastor Tom was holding the microphone and smiling as he approached, and the entire church erupted in excitement, especially the ushering team and the youth group, where he was an active member. He was grateful to them all. He heard about the vigil and knew the church had consistently upheld him in prayer daily for the last two months.

And God had answered. Not only had he come out of the initial danger, but he had left the hospital faster than the doctors had predicted, and here he was, back to his old self; apart from a few scars that indicated where he'd been stabbed, there was nothing else that showed the horror he'd been through.

"My name is John Griffith Jr., and I am standing here today to give God the glory and praise for sparing my life. Most of you know that I was stabbed about two months ago, but I've never told the entire story of what transpired. On that night, as I fell to the ground, a man stood over me. His presence stopped the assailants from stabbing me further. That was the first miracle. As I lay on the sidewalk, unable to help myself and passing in and out of consciousness, he was there, watching over me, a total stranger; I had never seen him, but his presence seemed unusually comforting. He stayed by my side as the paramedics worked and rode with me to the hospital in the ambulance.

"Some of you doubtless already know that the doctors thought they lost me in the theatre. I recall waking up on the operating table and walking out of the theatre. From a window, I climbed to an incredible height. Looking down, the distant building lights were reminiscent of an airplane's view. Drawn by music, I continued to ascend and approached a grand gate; I followed the sound to discover the most magnificent choir I'd ever witnessed. They were numerous, splendidly dressed in white. They sang magnificently, and I stood mesmerised as I watched them. It was unlike anything I had heard before, so I decided to join them. I had not rehearsed with them, but I like to think that I sing well."

The church erupted in laughter. John Jr. laughed, too, and continued his story.

"I knew the song, so I thought, why not? For those who know me, I love singing, but I joined the ushering team because I found it challenging to keep up with the choir rehearsals several times a week."

Again, the church erupted in laughter. John Jr. glanced at his dad and caught him rolling his eyes in mock exasperation. He chuckled.

"But this choir was different and so beautiful to watch that if they allowed me to join them, I would readily attend as many rehearsals as required. As I approached, a man stopped me. It was the same strange man who had appeared on the scene while I was being stabbed. I said to him, 'I want to sing with the choir.' Thinking he needed to know my credentials, I added, I sing very well and play the drums, too."

He paused as the church laughed at the audacity with which he bragged. He waited as Pastor Tom held up his hand for silence.

"The man smiled and shook his head. He was refusing me entry. His refusal shocked me. But why? I asked. It made no sense. He didn't answer but looked away, and as I followed his gaze, I saw The Vine Church. This auditorium was full, as it is now, with people wailing and praying. There wasn't time to take in what was before me because suddenly, I was falling rapidly from a great height. I opened my mouth to scream, but I landed on my back on the operating table, and the pain was so intense that it felt like my body had shattered into a thousand pieces. When I opened my eyes, after what seemed like a minute but had to be hours, I saw the same man by my bed in the recovery room.

"Brethren, I do not need to tell you that God saved me. I stand here as a testament to God, answering the church's prayers. He not only saved my life in response to your prayers but granted me a speedy recovery and healed me completely. And as I end my testimony, I quote from Revelations chapter five and verse thirteen, and I say, blessing, and honour, and glory, and power, be unto Him that sits upon the throne, and unto the Lamb forever and ever. Amen."

As John Jr. walked away from the altar and towards his seat, Rebekah, who was home from university for the weekend, stood up and pulled him in for a hug. Happy tears streamed down her face. John turned to look at his wife, who was sitting on his left-hand side; she, too, had tears running down her cheeks. He squeezed her hand, which was still linked in his, and with his right hand, he pulled out a handkerchief from his suit pocket and offered it to her. Their eyes met and held. So much had changed in the last two months since John Jr.'s near-fatal stabbing.

He had been spending more time with his family for one thing. Almost losing his son made him appreciate his wife and kids more and never take them for granted. He prayed for a long time with them, but he knew nothing was guaranteed, so he treasured every minute, every hour, and every day.

They'd been unable to travel, as John Jr. was recuperating, but they enjoyed a one-week staycation before the summer ended and school resumed. His love for Victoria, he thought, couldn't grow beyond what it was when they married, but he was wrong. He'd also come to appreciate her for holding down the fort while he cared for the sheep. Though he still cared for the sheep, he now did so with Victoria and other pastors sharing the burden. Including Victoria in his work improved their relationship. He watched his wife flourish and become more confident as he assigned her duties within the church.

She wasn't the only woman who had flourished in the last two months. Mabel was positively glowing. She had gone to Lagos for her wedding, after which she and her husband had a civil marriage ceremony in London and a church blessing at The Vine Church. They'd gone away for a honeymoon, and they still seemed to be in honeymoon mode as they couldn't keep their hands off each other.

Elizabeth, too, was glowing. Chris had moved back home and relaunched his real estate development business. God had been gracious to him as Princewill Consortium was already set to start building its first residential estate in Lagos. Elizabeth had confided in him only a few days ago that she was pregnant and taking an extended leave of absence from work to enable her to focus on her family. She was a woman in love. He had never seen her like that.

Audrey Campbell had stepped out of her role as the church's women leader. Her son Oliver had been killed on the night John Jr. was stabbed. The investigation into his murder uncovered many problems, and when it was revealed that he was responsible for John Jr.'s stabbing, Audrey suffered a heart attack. She was recovering but had been taken abroad to Saint Lucia by her husband. They planned to be gone for a couple of years to help her recover and also to help them heal from the loss of their youngest son.

With Audrey gone, the role of women leader was vacant, and although he hadn't told Victoria, the pastors had unanimously voted for her to succeed Audrey Campbell. They thought that with her children doing well in the ways of the Lord, and academically and with her calm inner strength, she had much to teach women and would be a good role model. Pastor Tom thought she embodied what a godly woman and wife ought to be. He agreed. He understood, from the number of pastors' ministries wrecked by their spouses, that his own spouse was exceptional. Victoria looked up from dabbing her eyes, and their eyes again met.

I love you, he mouthed and lifted her hand to his lips.

The End.

ABOUT ETURUVIE EREBOR

British by birth and Nigerian by descent, Eturuvie 'Evie' Erebor is an inspirational and self-growth speaker, writer, publisher, talk show host, and lawyer. She has written twenty-two books and published her article series, 'Preparing to Cleave', on the Vanguard Newspaper's Christian page in Nigeria between 2004 and 2007. Her articles have also been published in various newsletters and magazines, as well as on FaithWriters.Com.

Since 2004, she's spoken in churches and schools, transforming the lives of women and youth. Due to personal experience, she's determined to add more value to the lives of her fellow women. Hence, she began her initiative, 'DOZ Network'—writing and publishing DOZ Magazine, DOZ Devotional, and DOZ Chronicles, as well as hosting DOZ Show and DOZ Live Inspirational Conference.

A passionate storyteller, she's currently working on stories that appeal to women who are romantics at heart, and aid in her lifelong mission to educate, inspire, and empower with everything she does.

ABOUT DOZ CHRONICLES

DOZ Magazine was created to publish the stories of women, some painful, some joyful but all inspirational. When DOZ Magazine began operations in 2009, our true stories comprised a section within the magazine. However, readers quickly grew tired of reading the stories piece by piece. They came to loathe the phrase "to be continued", so we created an independent magazine dedicated to telling our inspirational stories in their entirety in a series. This magazine was known as the DOZ (True Story) Magazine, which significantly affected readers. It went out of circulation for a few years, but due to popular demand, it returned in 2015 as DOZ Chronicles. Under this title, four novellas were published, namely, DOZ Chronicles: Kemi, DOZ Chronicles: Lara, DOZ Chronicles: Ruki, and DOZ Chronicles: Nneka. They were published under the African Women Narratives series, and each is based on actual events.

The vision of DOZ Chronicles is expanding with its first fiction novel, DOZ Chronicles: Oloi.

Made in the USA
Columbia, SC
24 June 2025